VIKING SOCIETY TEXTS

GENERAL EDITORS

ALISON FINLAY AND CARL PHELPSTEAD

BISHOPS IN EARLY ICELAND

BISHOPS IN EARLY ICELAND

HUNGRVAKA
THE SAGA OF BISHOP PÁLL JÓNSSON
AN ACCOUNT OF THE PEOPLE AT ODDI
THE PRIESTHOOD OF BISHOP GUÐMUNDR GÓÐI

TRANSLATED BY
THEODORE M. ANDERSSON

VIKING SOCIETY FOR NORTHERN RESEARCH
UNIVERSITY COLLEGE LONDON
2021

© Viking Society for Northern Research
London 2021

ISBN: 978-1-914070-01-3

Cover Image: Bishop Guðmundr, from a sixteenth-century altarpiece containing a statue of Saint Óláfr from the church at Vatnsfjörður in the Westfjords. Photograph courtesy of the National Museum of Iceland.

Printed by Short Run Press Limited, Exeter

CONTENTS

PREFACE..vi
INTRODUCTION...vii
HUNGRVAKA (FORETASTE)...1
THE SAGA OF BISHOP PÁLL JÓNSSON...........................35
AN ACCOUNT OF THE PEOPLE AT ODDI......................65
THE PRIESTHOOD OF BISHOP GUÐMUNDR GÓÐI.......89
BIBLIOGRAPHY..155
INDEX OF PERSONAL NAMES..158
INDEX OF PLACE NAMES...171

PREFACE

The four translations assembled here are intended to supplement the early bishops' sagas that are already easily available in translation. All four of the present texts have been dated to the first years of the thirteenth century, *Hungrvaka* and *Páls saga byskups* with rather more certainty than the other two. Together with *Þorláks saga byskups*, which appeared in a translation by Ármann Jakobsson and David Clark in this series in 2013, and *Jóns saga helga*, which has recently appeared in a translation by Margaret Cormack, *The Saga of St. Jón of Hólar* (2021), these texts have been taken to typify the first emergence of saga writing and they show how the evolution of saga composition began. Students who begin by reading the more popular sagas about early Icelanders and the kings' sagas may be led to think of the 1220s as the period of emergence and the first blossoming of the sagas, but the first bishops' sagas offer a counterpoise and provide a distinctive picture of Icelandic culture shortly after 1200.

My first three translations are based on the editions by Ásdís Egilsdóttir in *Biskupa sögur* II (Reykjavík: Hið Íslenzka Fornritafélag, 2002). In that volume *Oddaverja þáttr* is printed as part of redaction B of *Þorláks saga bykups* (pp. 62–181). The chapter headings are my own. *Prestssaga Guðmundar góða* is translated from *Sturlunga saga*, ed. Jón Jóhannesson, Magnús Finnbogason, and Kristján Eldjárn (Reykjavík: Sturlunguútgáfan, 1946), vol. 1, 116–159.

I have not previously dealt with the bishops' sagas and owe a considerable debt to colleagues who have helped me along. I am grateful to Alison Finlay for giving these translations a home and patiently converting my spelling. I am also deeply indebted to Anthony Faulkes for the great labour he has put into the preparation of my manuscript for publication. Finally, I am beholden to Ásdís Egilsdóttir for help on a couple of passages that tested the limits of my Icelandic.

T. M. A.
July, 2021

The Early Icelandic Bishops

Skálaholt		Hólar	
Ísleifr Gizurarson	1056–1080	Jón Qgmundarson	1106–1121
Gizurr Ísleifsson	1082–1118	Ketill Þorsteinsson	1122–1145
Þorlákr Runólfsson	1118–1133	Bjǫrn Gilsson	1147–1162
Magnús Einarsson	1134–1148	Brandr Sæmundarson	1163–1201
Klœngr Þorsteinsson	1152–1175	Guðmundr Arason	1203–1237
Þorlákr Þórhallsson	1178–1193		
Páll Jónsson	1195–1211		

INTRODUCTION

HUNGRVAKA (FORETASTE)

The little treatise *Hungrvaka* is a good point of departure because it seems to be designed as an introduction, especially in the first and last chapters. It is clearly intended for readers who want to know more; in effect it is for beginners. This outlook is followed by an apologetic note about the book's brevity, and in turn by the somewhat contradictory claim that it nonetheless represents everything that the author is able to remember from his informants. That there was in fact a great deal more to be told is vouchsafed by the fuller accounts in the other bishops' sagas. The author allows for this greater inclusiveness by formulating the customary humility topos in such a way as to encourage later corrections and supplements.

The envisioned readers are specified as young men seeking to familiarise themselves with Icelandic materials. Whether this means that the intended readership is too young to have good Latin is not stated but might be surmised. The project is in any case educational in nature and seeks to inform the young readers about the growth of Christianity as an institution and the figures who were most important in its evolution. The readers of this volume will discover that education is a constant concern in all the texts collected here and that Christianity was as much an educational revolution as a religious one. The author wishes to write about 'how the church was founded and developed in Skálaholt', and this intention reveals a new attention to history as well. The study of history in Iceland, beginning with Ari Þorgilsson's *Íslendingabók* (Book about the Icelanders), will certainly also have had a role in focusing the outlook in the later sagas about Norwegian kings and early Icelanders as well, but in *Hungrvaka* the interest in history is explicit.

That *Hungrvaka* presents itself as a first introduction has not facilitated our dating of the text appreciably. Scholars seem fairly well agreed that the earliest bishops' sagas (*Þorláks saga*, *Jóns saga helga* and *Hungrvaka*) were all written in the first decade of the thirteenth century, but the exact order in which they were written has been much debated.[1] This is the point at which the final chapter of *Hungrvaka*

---

[1] Ásdís Egilsdóttir reviews the dating in *Biskupa sögur* II (2002), XXIV–XXXI.

comes into play. The last paragraph formulates a comparison between the bishops reviewed in *Hungrvaka* and Bishop Þorlákr Þórhallsson, much to the advantage of the latter: 'But however well the story of each of them [the early bishops] speaks of them, there is no fairer account in every respect than there is of the precious friend of God, Bishop Þorlákr, of whom it may rightly be said that he is the shining beam and gemstone of saints both in this country and everywhere in the world.' The words I have translated as 'fairer account' are *dæmi fegri*. *Dæmi* has a range of meanings from 'example' to 'testimony' to 'narrative'. Finnur Jónsson suspected that the words are not original and had been inserted by a scribe working on a manuscript in which *Þorláks saga* followed *Hungrvaka*, but the heavy emphasis on Þorlákr overall suggests that the words are part of the original.[1] If that is the case, the author of *Hungrvaka* must have been acquainted with a version, presumably written, of *Þorláks saga*, which is dated *c.* 1200.[2] *Hungrvaka* must therefore be a little later, perhaps as much as a decade. That still places it near the dawn of saga writing.

As a composition *Hungrvaka* suffers from a certain repetitive uniformity, which allowed the most recent editor, Ásdís Egilsdóttir, to draw up a seven-point template of each bishop's career:[3]

1. The bishop's genealogy and birth.
2. The bishop's physique and appearance.
3. His election and consecration.
4. His return to Iceland and initial activities.
5. His governance and routine, in particular his attention to the church at Skálaholt.
6. The approach of death.
7. An annalistic account of the important events in his time.

The monotony of this outline is reinforced by the uniformly eulogistic tone of the biographical sketches. There are no bad bishops, only pious and deeply committed ones. The early ones, Ísleifr (1056–1080) and his son Gizurr (1082–1118), have a certain legendary status, and Magnús Einarsson (1134–1148) emerges as one of the author's favourites. This does not mean that there are no questions at all about

[1] Finnur Jónsson, *OOLH* (1920–1924), vol. 2, 561.
[2] On the dating of *Þorláks saga* see the introduction to the translation by Ármann Jakobsson and David Clark (2013), vii–ix.
[3] See her 'Formáli' in *Biskupa sögur* II (2002), XX.

some of the bishops. Bishop Þorlákr Runólfsson (1118–1133) seems not to have been as personally prepossessing as some of the others. He is not credited with being handsome or of deep intelligence, and when he goes to Norway to be consecrated, the initial reaction is that there must not have been much to choose from in Iceland. Only an expression of special humility saves the day for him.

The most interesting case may be that of Klœngr Þorsteinsson (1152–1176), who is the last to be discussed and was presumably still in living memory. This memory was sufficiently alive to include a critical judgment of his extravagant spending, but the text nonetheless reassures us that God provides.[1] This is reminiscent of the mysterious provision of supplies at Bishop Guðmundr Arason's first Christmas in office, a story that has miraculous overtones in *Prestssaga Guðmundar góða*.[2] Apart from his extravagance, Bishop Klœngr is portrayed as a very exceptional figure in the tradition of his predecessors.

In light of the praise heaped on all of these personalities, the reader may despair of having any access to the reality behind the eulogies. The personal descriptions may nonetheless tell us a good deal about what qualities Icelanders in the first decade of the thirteenth century thought that a bishop should have. There is in the first place a great profusion of complimentary adjectives. They can be summarised as follows:

> Bishop Ísleifr: handsome, popular, just, upright, generous, benevolent
> Bishop Gizurr: tall, of noble appearance, strong, benevolent, of keen intelligence, fit to bear any title, commanding (in the sense that everyone is readily submissive), fit to be king or bishop
> Bishop Þorlákr Runólfsson: intelligent, well-behaved, well-disposed toward all good people, of quick intelligence, gentle, humble, unaggressive, helpful, benevolent, soft-spoken, compassionate, close to kin, restrained, loving toward a foster-child
> Bishop Magnús Einarsson: most beloved among siblings, handsome, tall (etc.), kindly, agreeable, very imposing in demeanour and courtesy, engaging, humble, generous, steadfast, competent, loyal, well-informed, well-spoken, conciliatory

[1] See below, p. 28.
[2] See below, p. 146.

Bishop Klœngr Þorsteinsson: handsome, of medium height, lively, possessed of a good presence, a good writer, very learned, a good speaker, steady, a great skald, generous, liberal, outgoing, gentle, humble, even-tempered, cheerful, witty, helpful

There is a certain variety in these characteristics, but there is also a real consistency in the focus of the qualities they describe. The approbation falls into two larger categories: details of a winning appearance and details of a winning manner. In effect they describe the qualities that make the bishops good leaders but also enable them to be on good terms with their flock. The focus is on social qualities. This focus distinguishes the bishops' sagas rather sharply from the kings' sagas and the sagas about early Icelanders. Neither of the latter narrative types devotes much attention to the amenable qualities of the main characters. The difference can surely be explained by the historical remoteness in time of the native sagas and the spatial remoteness of the Norwegian kings. The Icelanders did not need to interact with either group directly and had no reason to form an opinion about the sociability of their distant ancestors or of the remote kings. On the other hand, they were in close contact, direct or indirect, with their bishops, as the following texts will illustrate. The social niceties in dealing with bishops were important, and successful bishops were able to interact amicably with their countrymen. That requirement might explain the emphasis on engaging personalities in *Hungrvaka*.

It has already been noted that education is an important concern in *Hungrvaka*. At the outset Christian learning had to be acquired abroad, where a Christian culture was already in place. Both Ísleifr and Gizurr seem to have been trained in Saxony, and the foreign bishops who visit Iceland for longer or shorter periods in chapter 3 during Ísleifr's episcopacy brought Christian training with them. Bishop Jón was an Irishman, Bishop Bjarnvarðr Vilráðsson was alleged by some to be an Englishman, Bishop Rúðólfr came from a family in Rouen, and Bishop Bjarnvarðr was Saxon and had Norwegian experience. But beginning with Bishop Þorlákr Runólfsson, the Icelandic church seems to have made enough progress to be able to train its own clergy. We are told specifically that Bishop Þorlákr was educated at Haukadalr. Concerning Bishop Magnús Einarsson we are told simply that he 'was set to the task of studying and passed through all the orders before he became a priest'. In the case of Bishop

Klœngr Þorsteinsson the matter of education is omitted altogether. Whether education is mentioned or not, all the bishops have superior intellects. When Bishop Ísleifr returns to Iceland from Herford, he is described as well educated (*vel lærðr*). His son Gizurr is credited with a 'keen intelligence' (*forvitri*). Bishop Þorlákr, despite later doubts, is introduced in the first instance as 'intelligent at an early age' (*snemmendis skynsamr*). Bishop Magnús is 'well-informed' (*margfróðr*), and Bishop Klœngr is 'a very learned man' *(inn mesti lærdómsmaðr).*

This is not to say that there was no tradition of learning before the advent of Christianity in Iceland and the presence of scholars of great repute such as Sæmundr Sigfússon (1056–1133), but education was not an attribute of kings down to the time of Sverrir Sigurðarson (1184–1202), who had some clerical training, and Hákon Hákonarson (1217–1263), who is said to have had literary interests. When learning is mentioned in the sagas about early Icelanders, it is apt to refer to learning in the law, as in *Gunnlaugs saga* or *Njáls saga.* With the arrival of Christianity the definition is radically altered and comes to mean book learning, that is to say, familiarity with the Scriptures, saints' lives, homilies, and the like. It is the bishops' sagas that best mark this transition. There develops a distinction between those who are learned and those who are not, the learned and the lewd, and the bishops are the best representatives of the former. The twofold division of the population is made explicit during the episcopacy of Bishop Gizurr when the author remarks: 'It was also the view of all prudent men that by dint of benevolence and his [Gizurr's] own achievements he was the most distinguished man in Iceland, both among clerical and secular men.'

Another symptom of the redrawn ideological map in the bishops' sagas is the greatly expanded attention to death. It is remarkable how little space is allotted to death in the kings' sagas and the sagas about early Icelanders. This is partly because death in these sagas is more often than not a quick, violent death in battle, whereas in the bishops' sagas death tends to be the culmination of a slow and protracted illness, but this is not the only explanation. There is a ceremonial quality to the death scenes in the bishops' sagas. Death becomes a further test of the victim's fortitude and patience, an opportunity for the bishop to enhance his distinction and for others to demonstrate their compassion, in other words, an opportunity to reinforce Christian values. The new descriptive vocabulary and the new endurance in the face of death set these sagas apart from the rest of medieval Icelandic literature.

As we have seen, the biographical sketches in *Hungrvaka* suffer from a certain serial uniformity. We may nonetheless ask whether there are any overarching themes or preoccupations that characterise the text as a whole. One such concern might be the friction between the bishops and the general population that was not yet thoroughly committed to the rules of Christianity. This theme is sounded in chapter 2 when we are told that Bishop Ísleifr 'had great trouble in many respects because of people's disobedience,' and it is sounded again in the last sentence of the booklet, this time with reference to Bishop Þorlákr Þórhallsson: 'He [Bishop Þorlákr] may truly be called the apostle of Iceland just as Saint Patrick is called the apostle of Ireland, for they accomplished the work of the apostles themselves in their teaching and patience with disobedient and wrong-minded men.' The history of the Icelandic bishops might therefore to some extent be viewed as the history of the imposition of Christian rule on an only partially willing Icelandic population. The theme is not much emphasised in the booklet as a whole, but there are hints here and there. Immediately after the sentence from chapter 2 quoted above we learn that certain foreign bishops became popular because of their greater leniency. The Icelandic bishops therefore confronted not only unreceptive countrymen but rival bishops as well. The resistance is reaffirmed in the same chapter when Ísleifr tells the Icelanders that they will have a hard time finding a successor unless they are more accommodating toward him than they have been toward Ísleifr himself.

His son Gizurr seems indeed to be a reluctant successor and agrees only when 'all the chieftains promised him to be submissive to all of God's ordinances.' Gizurr turns out in fact to be extraordinarily successful, and we are told that 'everybody wished to do exactly as he ordered,' but it sounds as though that is precisely the opposite of what might be expected. In chapter 5 Bishop Þorlákr Runólfsson turns out to be an equally reluctant candidate. That must be understood as part and parcel of the humility expected of a nominee for bishop, but the job may nonetheless have been daunting, and it is regularly referred to as 'the difficulty' or 'the difficulties.' After the death of Bishop Gizurr we are told about a period of hostility and lawlessness (p. 16). At the end of chapter 7 we learn something about the difficulties encountered by Þorlákr Runólfsson: 'Many chieftains were unmanageable in their dealings with Bishop Þorlákr because of their disobedience, in some cases dishonest dealing and crime, but he controlled everything as best he could.'

The resistance in the general population is not a constant concern in *Hungrvaka*, but it will become a central problem especially in *An Account of the People of Oddi* and *The Priesthood of Guðmundr the Good* below. It is clear that the tension between ecclesiastic interests and secular interests was an endemic problem in Iceland.

THE SAGA OF BISHOP PÁLL JÓNSSON

Unlike the general run of bishops' sagas, *Páls saga* has a dramatic structure. One departure from the norm is that it is not burdened by a long sequence of miracles, which, in *Þorláks saga biskups* and *Jóns saga helga*, tend to blur the biographical thrust of the story. *Páls saga* focuses on a remarkable individual without detracting from the story with an episodic aftermath. In addition, the narrative has real shape. Páll and his wife at first live in narrow circumstances, but such are their skills and such is the good will of their friends that they soon become prosperous—'and their property grew like the sea washing onto the shore.' It may seem anomalous that a bishop-to-be is singled out for his worldly wealth, but Ásdís Egilsdóttir has pointed out that Páll's exceptional patience is modelled on the proverbial patience of Job.[1] We might carry the analogy further and suggest that Páll's influx of wealth is an understated reminiscence of Job's 'seven thousand sheep, three thousand camels, five hundred yoke of oxen and five hundred she-donkeys' (Job 1.3). His early good fortune is expressly noted near the beginning of chapter 12: 'Bishop Páll was such a fortunate man that everything turned to his advantage in the early part of his life.' But, as in Job's case, the great wealth and the blessings that come with it are illusory. Both Job and Páll begin with immeasurable good fortune only to succumb to great misery. The first stage of Job's fall from grace is the fiery death of his sons and daughters (Job 1.18–19). Páll's catastrophe is the drowning of his wife Herdís and his daughter Halla. In the Book of Job Satan is unrelenting, but in *Páls saga* God tries to moderate the affliction. As the text says (p. 54) 'it

---

[1] See her edition (2002), CXXVII.

seemed to everyone that God had reckoned very narrowly what he [Páll] could bear.' To some extent Páll is able to conceal his grief in order to carry out his duties. Some people are fooled, but the author knows better (p. 54): 'But everyone may find it more likely that his patience was the explanation, and his wish to honour people with his kindness rather than that his sorrow diminished as long as he lived.' Páll thus lives a life of great privilege and contentment in his early years but in the shadow of his wife's death in his last four years. The author has succeeded in constructing not just a neutral biography but also a gripping tale of misfortune. At the center of the tale is Herdís, and we will see presently what the implications of her central position may be. We do not know who the author of the saga was, but the text offers a rather detailed profile of what the author's interests were. He is clearly interested in Herdís, although he provides only her father's name and gives her a positive but somewhat perfunctory introduction at the outset—'a fair woman and accomplished in all matters that are a credit to women.' But there is a paragraph devoted to her competence at the end of the first chapter. While Páll studies abroad, she is left to manage the household and bring up their four children. This she does so well that no children in the whole district are considered to be so well brought up (p. 40): 'That remained the case for as long as she lived, for she was the most exacting of women both with respect to herself and others, as often proved true.' This is a quite remarkable passage because the raising of children is not commonly mentioned in the sagas and we would be hard put to find a counterpart. But that is not her exclusive competence. At the end of chapter 4 there is another paragraph that signals her abilities. When Páll is installed at Skálaholt, she comes to preside and is of equal assistance to him personally and in his official church capacity. The text tells us explicitly that no one was her match (p. 40). This is particularly impressive because she is in charge of close to two hundred residents. The refrain is taken up again in the last paragraph of chapter 12: 'Herdís secured all those things that the estate needed with her intelligence and supervision and all necessary activity in such a way that she was the most precise in every function among all those who were there on this estate and all the other properties that the bishop owned.' The irony of her competence is that the immediate cause of her death is her eagerness to cross a flooded river in order to get home to take care of business. It is small wonder then that the day of her death is held in special reverence (p. 54): 'It was the custom of many people, both laymen and clerics, to remember her as earnestly and lovingly as their nearest relatives because of her manifold solicitude.' The author also takes more than the average interest in Bishop Páll's children. They are not only well brought up and promising but they fulfill their promise. After the drowning of Herdís and her daughter Halla, the second daughter Þóra takes over the domestic management, even though she is only fourteen years of age (p. 54)—'she managed so well that those who were best acquainted with her admired her ways most of all.' But even before that the individual accomplishments of the four children are taken account of (p. 52). Loptr is outstanding in skill and learning and wisdom, Ketill excels in judgment and handwriting, while Þóra is good-natured and affectionate. All four are celebrated in a stanza by Ámundi the Smith, and this may well be the only Old Icelandic stanza dedicated to four children. It looks like a case of adults identifying the best qualities in their children and certainly suggests a strong family consciousness. The idea of a close-knit family emerges indirectly when King Sverrir receives Páll in Norway 'as if it were his son or brother visiting him' (p. 40). There is in fact more focus on family life and home life in this bishop's saga than there is in the misnamed family sagas. Special mention is made of the death of Páll's father, Jón Loptsson, the greatest chieftain in Iceland, and the ensuing loss of family support for Páll. The emphasis on the prosperity of Páll and Herdís may not be so much a comment on their worldly success as on their domestic and managerial abilities. Their abilities carry over to their children and therefore become a family focus. So too is the matter of education. Páll goes abroad to hone his intellectual accomplishments (pp. 37–38): 'When he came back to Iceland, he outdid everyone else in his learned accomplishments, his command of verse, and his knowledge of book learning.' We know from *Landnámabók* that Herdís's brother Ketill was a priest and that may suggest that she too was exposed to some form of clerical culture.[1] Book learning is mentioned specifically in the case of three out of four children, Loptr, Ketill, and Halla (p. 52). Practical household abilities apparently went along with more bookish skills. To some extent the text thus gives us

---

[1] See *Landnámabók* (1968), vol. 2: 382, n.2.

access to family-wide traditions and accomplishments, but the author is also at pains to give each family member an individual personality. Each member is marked by a particular skill and a particular character trait. Thus Páll is deeply learned as his office requires, but he is also remarkable for his Job-like patience, his moderation, and his peaceable disposition. Herdís is a high-energy businesswoman, but she also exhibits a touching solicitude for a household of nearly two hundred staff and workers, and it is for this quality that she is mourned. Among the children Loptr combines learning skills with the more mature quality of wisdom. Ketill combines the somewhat rudimentary skill of handwriting with the rare gift of good judgment. Halla combines the household skill of handiwork with the more intellectual achievement of book learning. Þóra is initially praised only for her capacity for 'accommodation and affection,' which are personal qualities, but after the death of her mother and sister she demonstrates that she too has the practical capability of taking over the household. In this way the author is able to project clearly defined and rounded characters. It should be said that the author seems to have greater interest in the private sphere than in the public sphere. Bishop Páll is praised for his chieftainly support of his followers, but no specifics are provided. Public controversy is the very stuff of the sagas about early Iceland, but such matters are passed over in silence. Together with other chieftains Páll introduces a standard measuring rod, but this seems a little trivial. Perhaps the most neglected public arena is the struggle between the newly appointed bishop at Hólar, Guðmundr Arason, and the local chieftains in the north. This conflict has the most dramatic implications for Bishop Páll because he has a direct order from the Norwegian archbishop to assist his colleague at Hólar, but at the same time he finds himself allied with some of the northern chieftains who oppose Guðmundr. This is the sort of impasse treated at great length by the later bishops' sagas, but for the author of *Páls saga* the situation becomes not a subject of highly charged conflict, only an opportunity to display Bishop Páll's reasonableness and spirit of compromise. It is once more the private sphere that prevails. There is an interesting overlap between Bishop Páll's domestic sphere and his ecclesiastical sphere. The church estate seems in some measure to be an extension of Páll's residence. His wife Herdís manages not only his personal interests but the ecclesiastical estate as a whole; she has both a private and a public function. Páll shares this dual responsibility. As soon as he is installed, he undertakes to complete the building improvements that Bishop Þorlákr had contemplated. After his consecration in Norway he returns to Iceland with two glass windows to ornament his church (p. 42), but his greatest enterprise is the construction of a splendid new bell tower, which he defrays to some extent with his own private means in the amount of four hundred hundreds (p. 44). The particulars of the construction are provided in detail, both architectural and artistic. The saga as a whole in fact has a strong artisanal focus. In chapter 8 Páll commissions an elaborate and very precious coffin for Bishop Þorlákr with another outlay of four hundred hundreds, and in chapter 16 he commissions an ornately carved ivory staff as a gift for Archbishop Þórir and a similarly ornate altarpiece for his own church. In general Páll undertakes to make his church the most spectacular sight in Iceland, 'to adorn the church still more than before after he was consecrated, even though it was already more finely and splendidly adorned than any other church in Iceland' (p. 43). In his new bell tower he houses an (additional?) church, which 'he adorned . . . beautifully in every respect' (p. 44). We are given details of the painted ceiling, the wall hangings, and the burial monuments. There is an almost museum-like quality to the undertaking, and there is talk of 'pictures and crosses, tablets, paintings, lamps and glass windows, and episcopal adornments of all kinds' (p. 45). This is all clearly intended to attract viewers and raise the profile of the church. It is surely no coincidence that 'a great multitude,' including several important personages, assembles to witness Bishop Páll's first celebration of Mass (p. 43). There is an issue of public appeal as well as religious participation.

Páls saga is certainly the most decorative of the bishops' sagas, but the reader may find it difficult to decide whether the ornamentation reflects Páll's own artistic orientation or the author's elaboration of his investment in art. The details are striking enough to suggest at the very least that the author shared the bishop's artistic aspirations. That bishop and author were close to each other is indicated by a number of factors. The saga is not a dry report but a quite personal account with not a few hints that the author was a close acquaintance of the family. He is thoroughly familiar not only with the decorative objects but with the inner workings of the household. He knows Páll himself well but Herdís and her children perhaps even better. He also knows the staff, not only the names and functions but their personalities as well, and he devotes a separate chapter (14) to the men in Páll's service. He seems to have been present at, or to have known at first hand about, crucial events. The gripping scene of Herdís's and Halla's drowning is resurrected in such painful detail that it would not be surprising to learn that the author was an eyewitness. He also knows the prelude to Bishop Páll's death and who was present at his deathbed. He knows that Páll got back to Skálaholt exactly three days before Saint Simon's Day, and he knows the exact sequence of symptoms prior to Páll's death. These are matters that could have been relayed to him by others, but it is perhaps easier to imagine that he was in the household himself and knew the facts firsthand.

Sveinbjörn Rafnsson has made a detailed case for believing that Bishop Páll's son Loptr was the author of the saga sometime between 1229 and 1235.[1] That would place the saga twenty years after the bishop's death in 1211. To the present reader it seems that the events of the story are recorded in very fresh memory and that the saga is quite likely to have been written soon after Páll's death. Loptr Pálsson's authorship either early or late (Sveinbjörn calculates that he was born *c.* 1190) seems perfectly possible, but, if so, he adopts an outsider's stance in discussing himself and his siblings. This stance seems more appropriate for someone very close to the family but not identical with one of the children. We surely need to think of someone who was much attached to Herdís and eager to preserve her memory but also had a strong interest in the children. Herdís's brother Jón is mentioned as being present at the drowning, but nothing more is said and he is not known from other sources.[2] He may have died young. Quite another matter is a second brother of Herdís's, Þorlákr. This brother was not present at the drowning, but he could have learned the details from Jón or from others who were eyewitnesses. Þorlákr was the son of a priest and the father of a priest.[3] There is therefore

---

[1] Sveinbjörn Rafnsson 1993, 33–40. In her edition Ásdís Egilsdóttir voiced some reservations (2002, CXXXI–CXXXII). In his edition Einar Ól. Sveinsson suggested that Bishop Páll's treasurer Þórir, mentioned in chapter 16, could have been the author (1954, 13). I will make another suggestion below.

[2] There was another Jón Ketilsson, a priest mentioned in *Guðmundar saga Arasonar*, ed. Guðni Jónsson, vol. 2, 213, but he died in 1192.

[3] See *Landnámabók* (1968), vol. 1, 147, 173 and vol. 2, 220, n. 2, 269, n. 4, 287, n. 12, 382, n. 2, and the genealogy XVII a. Þorlákr died in 1240.

no reason to doubt his religious sentiments or his book culture. Furthermore, he earns a special comment after the loss of Herdís in the following terms (p. 54): 'Bishop Páll lavished great comfort both in words and material gifts on Herdís's brother Þorlákr, and he honoured him in all respects no less than before he lost her. After her death he comforted Þorlákr no less than his own family' (p. 54).

This comment seems somewhat unmotivated in view of the fact that Þorlákr has no role whatever in the saga. It looks as though the writer may be using his authorial privilege to express a special message of gratitude to Bishop Páll. But what of Þorlákr's relationship to the children? Here too there may be a hint to help us along. In chapter 8 the author notes the special relationship that joins maternal uncles to their nephews and nieces (p. 47):

> Though great honour had already been accorded Bishop Páll, as was proper, even before the saintliness of Bishop Þorlákr was revealed, it redounded much to his credit that he had a truly outstanding maternal uncle, and many people considered that the old saying was borne out stating that men most resemble their maternal uncles.

Perhaps the author is suggesting that just as Bishop Þorlákr stood his nephew Páll in good stead, so Herdís's brother Þorlákr stands his nephews and nieces in good stead. There must have been other uncles in the picture, including the mysterious Jón, and we might wonder why Þorlákr is singled out. He may have been a favourite uncle, or perhaps he was particularly attached to his nephews and nieces. In any event, an uncle living in the larger household would seem to be a good candidate for the author of a biography. He would have been close to all the family members and would have been familiar with all the inner workings of the residence. He may also have had a particularly close relationship to his sister Herdís, who figures so prominently in the story. The identifying of an anonymous author is probably a vain undertaking, but perhaps we might say that the author of *Páls saga* was someone like Þorlákr Ketilsson.

AN ACCOUNT OF THE PEOPLE AT ODDI (ODDAVERJA ÞÁTTR)

The text that goes under this title is found in redactions B and C of *Þorláks saga* but not in redaction A. Apart from brief mentions in literary histories it has not been much discussed until quite recently. In

1968 Jón Böðvarsson noted a consensus that the author of redaction A had suppressed everything about the disputes between Bishop Þorlákr and the people at Oddi and other chieftains, and that would of course have included *Oddaverja þáttr*.[1] The change may have been effected out of deference to Bishop Páll Jónsson and his Oddi connections. Jón Böðvarsson himself took a different view and considered redaction B to be a corrective to redaction A, written as late as the days of Bishop Árni Þorláksson at the end of the thirteenth century (p. 92). He does not, however, speculate on how the narrative of *Oddaverja þáttr* came into existence, whether it was based on supplementary tradition or devised as a precedent for the disputes over church administration between bishops and landowners with private churches in the time of Bishop Árni. It will be argued here that the tale is traditional and evolved into a fully formed narrative that could have been interpolated into redaction B at any time in the thirteenth century. It was not an adjustment of redaction B but a complete story added into redaction B. Much of the recent discussion, notably in two papers by Ármann Jakobsson and Ásdís Egilsdóttir, has focused on the dating of the B version and the indications that it might be late. These scholars have noted the use of present participles, the form of address *herra* for bishops, and the use of direct discourse as late features.[2] There are also chronological errors, the most conspicuous of which is the marriage of Jón Loptsson's mistress Ragnheiðr to a Norwegian named Arnþórr and a resulting large progeny although she must at the very least have been forty-five years old and of declining fertility.[3] We are also told that Eyjólfr at Stafaholt did not live long after his encounter with Bishop Þorlákr, who died in 1193, but the annals tell us that he did

[1] Jón Böðvarsson 1968, 82.
[2] Ármann Jakobsson and Ásdís Egilsdóttir 1998 and 1999.
[3] Ármann Jakobsson and Ásdís Egilsdóttir 1998, 138 and 1999, 95. The conclusion of chapter 9 tells us that many people were descended from Ragnheiðr and Arnþórr, but that may not mean that they had many children. The numerous progeny may have accrued in the following generation or generations, and that would be a futher argument for a late interpolation of *Oddaverja þáttr.* Darrel Asmundsen and Carol Jean Diers (1973) showed that, as far as it goes, the medieval evidence suggests that menopause set in at about the same age then as now, around 50. Ragnheiðr may have had just one child by Arnórr and the increase in offspring may have occurred between 1220 and 1250.

not die until 1213.¹ Such miscalculations seem unlikely if *Oddaverja þáttr* were an early text, let us say from the 1220s. Also suspect is the emphasis on the church disputes between the landowners and Bishop Þorlákr in light of the fact that such disputes are not mentioned in other contemporary sources and are more consonant with the well-known disputes at the end of the century.² Not all these indications seem equally decisive, but they are certainly sufficient to raise doubts about an early date. At the same time critics seem reluctant to classify *Oddaverja þáttr* as a pure invention, and they seem to agree that it has some basis in tradition.³ They do not speculate on how it was added and exactly at what date, but there is a vivid contrast in style between *Þorláks saga* and *Oddaverja þáttr*. The saga is eulogistic and centred almost exclusively on the bishop. The *þáttr* is an exceptionally good example of saga style with scenic detail, tense confrontations, and a dramatic buildup. It seems quite unlikely that the biography and the action-packed *þáttr* are from the same hand. One clear difference is the heavy reliance on biblical quotations in the biography and the absence of a single quotation in *Oddaverja þáttr*. Equally striking is the contrast between the highly developed and often biting dialogue in the *þáttr* and the almost complete lack of dialogue in the biography, with the exception of a few pious exchanges when Bishop Þorlákr is on his deathbed. Like the sagas in general *Oddaverja þáttr* is a tale of sharply focused conflict, and the conflict is enhanced by acid dialogue with a possible recourse to arms not always unspoken. The encounters are prefaced by overland marches that give the reader time to ponder the outcome. Three times the outcome is artificially deferred by a mysterious fog that makes one contending party invisible to the other. The supernatural advent of fog is sometimes seen in the context of miracle literature, but the occurrences may be more reminiscent of the magical mists that arise in the classical sagas, for example in *Njáls saga*.⁴ They are for dramatic effect. In other ways too the text is reminiscent of saga narrative. The classical sagas are notoriously focused on legal issues, and that it is no less true of *Oddaverja þáttr*. It is constructed around the question of whether the churches on private

¹ Ármann Jakobsson and Ásdís Egilsdóttir 1999, 95–96.
² Ibid. 1998, 141 and 1999, 97.
³ Jon Böðvarsson 1968, 93; Orri Vésteinsson 2000, 113, 169.
⁴ See Ármann Jakobsson and Ásdís Egilsdóttir 1998, 139; *Njáls saga*, chapter 12 (ÍF 12, 38).

land are subject to secular or ecclesiastical authority, the so-called *staðamál*. Because the sagas are so preoccupied with legal issues, the dialogue often revolves around negotiations, controversies, or settlements.[1] The rich use of dialogue in *Oddaverja þáttr* conforms to this tradition.

The style of the *þáttr* echoes the sagas in a number of other respects. New characters are introduced with information on their ancestry, family connections, and prominent characteristics just as in the sagas. The introduction of the priest Hǫgni at the beginning of chapter 5 is a good case in point, even though he is not descended from a particularly distinguished family. The narrative as a whole develops as a series of confrontations between individuals. Bishop Þorlákr first confronts the chieftains in the East, then Jón Loptsson, then the priest Hǫgni, then Eyjólfr at Stafaholt, then for a second time Hǫgni, then Sveinn Sturluson, then Þorsteinn Jónsson, and the sequence culminates in an epic confrontation with Jón Loptsson himself. These encounters are not merely serial events but become increasingly fraught with danger in the tradition of saga escalation. Þorlákr's confrontations with Jón Loptsson and his son Þorsteinn at the end are in fact life-threatening. The bishop survives one threat by a miracle and the second by the last-moment desperate intervention of a follower and a razor-thin compromise. The last phase is also characterised by exceptional visual detail as Bishop Þorlákr and his men ride into a narrow passage between serried enemies as prearranged by Jón Loptsson. This episode is also reminiscent of the final stands staged by Icelandic saga heroes with dense depictions of time and space.

Along with these manipulations of tempo go certain anticipatory devices familiar from the art of saga writing, such as prophetic utterances and warnings of impending peril. Thus Þorsteinn Jónsson, toward the end of chapter 8, tells his father that he will rid him of the interference from Bishop Þorlákr, but Jón predicts that he will be discountenanced: 'You can meet with the bishop if you like, but you are destined to have quite a different misfortune other than convincing Þorlákr to do anything.' We therefore know in advance that Þorsteinn will fail; the only question is how he will fail. When Þorsteinn arrives on the scene, people warn Þorlákr to remain inside and not expose

---

[1] I emphasise this in 'A Note on Conversations in the Sagas,' *Gripla* 28 (2017), 227–235.

himself to his antagonist's weapons. Þorlákr rejects the advice and advances toward Þorsteinn's raised axe, but as Þorsteinn prepares to deliver the blow, his arm is suddenly paralysed and the bishop is spared. When Þorsteinn reports to his father on his misadventure, Jón replies with the dry comment: 'That is about what I thought would happen.' Sardonic understatement is also characteristic of the sagas.

Chapter 6 provides an even fuller example of anticipatory technique. Here a priest named Magnús accompanies Bishop Þorlákr along a route from Reykjaholt with a band of men. As they part, Magnús explains: 'Today I know that you will need reinforcement, and for that reason I took many men with me. I want to accompany you until I know that you are out of harm's way.' Þorlákr inquires into the nature of the danger and is told that the priest Hǫgni wishes to abduct him to his farm at Bœr and force him to consecrate his church. Þorlákr declines any further assistance and is indeed abducted, but his steadfastness proves more than a match for Hǫgni and he is allowed to proceed on his way. The motif of a doomed march with the offer and refusal of help is attested for example in *Laxdœla saga* as Kjartan approaches an ambush having turned down proffered companionship.[1] *Oddaverja þáttr* not only subscribes to the dramatic and escalatory practices of traditional saga-writing but also to an overall historical perspective suggesting the passage of considerable time. Thus Bishop Þorlákr's transfer of eastern churches to ecclesiastical authority at the end of chapter 3 ends with the words 'and that has remained in force ever since' (*ok þat hefir þar haldizk jafnan síðan*). The author is pondering events long past. At the beginning of the following chapter the author summarises Jón Loptsson's attention to church welfare and adds: 'He was also well versed in all the accomplishments practised by men at that time.' The phrase 'at that time' (*í þann tíma*) also suggests that a good deal of history has passed. At the end of chapter 4 there are two references to time long past, the first one alluding to Bishop Þorlákr's lack of success in other parts of the country: 'Others then followed the example of Jón and no one wished to surrender churches to the authority of Bishop Þorlákr, and that put an end to his claims during his time.' The phrase 'during his time' (*um hans daga*) establishes a certain time lapse between Jón Loptsson's era and the author's own era. Even the very last sentence of the text casts the time of Jón

---

[1] *Laxdœla saga*, chapters 48–49 (ÍF 5, 151–152).

Loptsson in historical terms: 'When he was gone, his sons divided the church and dismantled the buildings as their paternal inheritance, and the words of the holy bishop Þorlákr were revealed as they were recorded above.' The very landscape has changed during the time that separates the author of the *þáttr* from the events in Jón's lifetime. This historical perspective may be an additional factor in considering *Oddaverja þáttr* as a text set down in writing quite late. The comments above should suggest that the narrative techniques in *Oddaverja þáttr* associate it with the classical sagas, and the same may be said of the narrative shape as a whole. The central part of the story is formed as a gradually intensifying sequence of one-to-one encounters, and that is the very hallmark of saga composition. In addition, the conclusions of classical sagas tend to tail off into a few historical notices without dramatic impact. This is equally true of the *þáttr*. It moves quietly into Jón Loptsson's old age and decline and records a few nostalgic words addressed to his church. Apart from narrative and structural similarities to the classical sagas we might take note of the authorial posture. For the most part the bishops' sagas treat their protagonists in strictly laudatory terms, even the questionable character of Guðmundr Arason. By contrast, the author of *Oddaverja þáttr* adheres to saga precedent by casting the quarrel between Bishop Þorlákr and Jón Loptsson in quite neutral terms. Neither is a hero and neither is a villain. The sagas naturally have introductory conventions as well as agonistic and concluding conventions, but the former are not applicable in the case of *Oddaverja þáttr* since the scene has already been set in the preceding part of *Þorláks saga*. The opening chapters of the *þáttr* are nonetheless of special interest because they show how the text of the saga and the text of the *þáttr* were knit together. The passages translated below as chapters 1 and 2 may be to a considerable degree the work of the saga author, not the *þáttr* author. The first chapter is in the devotional style of the saga with three characteristic Bible quotations. Chapter 2 sums up the content of the saga ('the propitious conduct of this blessed bishop and no less of his episcopal authority and holy moderation') and retains the devout style, but it concludes with the words: 'And for that reason I will begin the story when he first came to Iceland as a bishop.' This is a duplication because the saga has already begun the story with an account of Þorlákr's birth and early years. The text thus has two beginnings; one belongs to the saga and the other to the *þáttr*. This

INTRODUCTION xxv

last sentence of chapter 2 marks the transition from one to the other, the point at which the writer interpolated the *þáttr*. For our purposes it is important to note that the *þáttr* has a clear beginning and a clear conclusion. It was conceived as a whole and interpolated as a whole. It should therefore be studied as a separate text. Guðni Jónsson clearly had a sense of this when he printed it as a separate text.[1]

Version B of *Þorláks saga* is generally thought to have been composed quite early,[2] but the *þáttr* is now thought to be quite late because of the perceived errors and the late stylistic traits. It is placed in the context of Bishop Árni Þorláksson's church disputes in the 1270s and 1280s. To the indications already brought forward I have added the somewhat distant temporal perspectives in *Oddaverja þáttr*. The *þáttr* could have been interpolated at any time between the 1220s and the 1280s, but if we believe that chapters 1 and 2 as they are printed here show the imprint of the original author's style, then we must believe that the *þáttr* was interpolated early and must therefore have been composed early. The only alternative would be to suppose that a late interpolator was very skilled at imitating the style of the original author. That seems to be a somewhat farfetched supposition. Let us consider for a moment the idea that the *þáttr* is late and that its chief characteristic is saga style. Saga style was of course equally possible at any time between 1220 and 1280. That is precisely the culminating era in saga composition. If we choose the early alternative, we must suppose that an independent writer opted to compose a saga on the controversy between Bishop Þorlákr and Jón Loptsson and cast it in saga style. The problem is of course that such a saga would be unique; saga authors did not cast near contemporaries as saga protagonists in what we recognise as saga style. The alternative explanation would be that the quarrel between Jón and the bishop lived on in oral tradition and evolved into a narrative in saga style before it was added into version B of *Þorláks saga biskups*. This process would also be anomalous because we do not normally imagine that events around 1200 became the stuff of saga writing. On the other hand Jón Loptsson was the most prominent figure in Iceland at the turn of the century and the most likely to be elaborated in memory. He is also the most likely secular person to

[1] The text is printed separately in the first volume of his *Byskupa sögur* (1953, 131–154).
[2] Jón Helgason, 'Þorláks saga helga' (1976, col. 390) suggests *c.* 1225 while noting that others prefer a later date.

have enjoyed equal status with the early bishops. There was presumably enough residual resentment of ecclesiastical authority to foster the status of a secular antagonist. Such resentment is explicit in the elaborately conceived saga of Guðmundr Arason, and there is an ample hint of it in the emphasis on moderation in *Páls saga biskups,* which, like *Oddaverja þáttr*, dramatises the inherent conflict between the letter of the law and reasonable accommodation. It remains to explain how this oral evolution into saga toward the end of the thirteenth century can be reconciled with the wording of the transitional narrative translated here as chapters 1 and 2, wording that seems to belong to the original author of version B in, let us suppose, the 1220s. Perhaps we can surmise that chapter 1 simply does not belong to the transitional wording but merely summarises the early phases of Þorlákr's spiritual development in preparation for the resumption of the main narrative in chapter 30 of Ásdís Egilsdóttir's edition (p. 181).The only true transitional prose is the very short chapter 2. Here it is only the first sentence that puts us in mind of the devotional tone in *Þorláks saga*:

> And now since something has been said of the propitious conduct of the blessed bishop and no less of his episcopal authority and holy moderation, it is appropriate to listen to the words and events that attest how fitting it was that Þorlákr had a shepherd's name and was eternally reckoned among those bishops who adhered to the laws of almighty God in the highest degree and did not spare themselves from the sword of persecution even though God, who is all-powerful, allots for their protection both roses and lilies for their praise and glory.[1]

This sentence betrays a heavy ecclesiastical hand and refers back to the immediately preceding paragraph at the end of chapter 1 about Þorlákr's 'governing power' and 'moderation'. But it does not necessarily belong to the original author of *Þorláks saga* and could be devised by a cleric toward the end of the century as he prepares to interpolate into his text part of the very 'little and limited material' to which he refers in the next sentence. The formidable gap between the style of the transitional sentence above and the style of

---

[1] On roses and lilies Ásdís Egilsdóttir in her edition (2002, XXXVII) refers us to Jonna Louis-Jensen, 'Om roser og liljer,' 2006, 53–55. Louis-Jensen understands the lilies to mean a pure life and the roses to suggest potential martyrdom.

Oddaverja þáttr, beginning in chapter 3, is another piece of evidence that the *þáttr* was available in complete written form and was simply interpolated into version B.

If it is true that *Oddaverja þáttr* developed orally through the thirteenth century and was added toward the end of the century, that is a significant supplement to our studies of the transition from oral transmission to written sagas. We generally think of two or three hundred years as the oral term before a saga appears in writing, but I have argued elsewhere that it may have taken only about a hundred years for a tradition to morph into a saga.[1] My best example was *Þorgils saga ok Hafliða*, reflecting events from around 1100 and formulated as a saga perhaps around 1220. On the other hand I know of no examples of narrative material from around 1200 appearing in full-blown saga form let us say around 1280. The closest analogy might be *Arons saga Hjǫrleifssonar*, which seems to have gone through an oral evolution from *c.* 1250 to *c.* 1350.[2] If *Oddaverja þáttr* is also a case of evolving oral transmission, it tells us that the mechanisms governing the passage of oral tradition into literary form were in full force during the thirteenth century.

THE PRIESTHOOD OF BISHOP GUÐMUNDR GÓÐI

The quite full saga about Bishop Guðmundr Arason confronts us with a number of problems, not least of all considerable uncertainty about the dating of the text. At one time it was attributed to Guðmundr's deacon Lambkárr Þorgilsson, a close associate of Guðmundr's. This is a particularly persuasive hypothesis because it emerges from the saga that Lambkárr had a very exact knowledge of Guðmundr's affairs. Chapter 24 of the saga tells us that Guðmundr was caught in a serious snowstorm and survived by finding a house together with two deacons, one of whom was Lambkárr. Lambkárr therefore figures as a close travelling companion and may have played that part on a regular basis. Guðmundr was a constant traveller, and the saga follows his peregrinations in detail and with a precise knowledge of the chronology. Not only that, but we are told in chapter 26 that Lambkárr was in charge of Guðmundr's papers: 'Before they got to Hólar, the deacon Lambkárr

---

[1] I make this argument in 'The Long Prose Form in Medieval Iceland' (2002).

[2] See Jónas Kristjánsson 1988, 201.

had always attended to the documents when Guðmundr was at home.' He therefore functioned as Guðmundr's private secretary and was a member of the inner circle. This privileged position, however, becomes a source of contention in the following sentence: 'But as soon as he [Lambkárr] got to Hólar, he was shunned in all secretarial matters and Kygri-Bjǫrn [Hjaltason] was put in charge of the documentation in his place.' The text goes on to say that a serious enmity grew up between Guðmundr and Kygri-Bjǫrn.

It sounds very much as though the author is allowing himself a moment of pique at being displaced by a rival. But at some point Lambkárr may have recovered his position. If he is indeed the author of *Prestssaga Guðmundar góða*, it is worth noting that in chapter 28 he cites no fewer than five letters: from Guðmundr to Sigurðr Ormsson, from Guðmundr to Bishop Páll Jónsson, from Páll Jónsson to Sæmundr Jónsson, from Sæmundr to Páll Jónsson, and from Páll Jónsson to Guðmundr. Who is more likely to have had access to an inventory of such documents than Guðmundr's secretary Lambkárr? The problem in assigning the authorship of the saga to Lambkárr is a chronological one. Lambkárr died in 1249, so that the earliest plausible date for his birth might be *c.* 1190. That would make him too young (about ten years old) to have been in Guðmundr's employ around 1200. It also seems unlikely that he would have had such detailed information about Guðmundr's life at such an early age. The particularly close-up description of Guðmundr's shipwreck in chapter 6, datable to the spring of 1180, is difficult to square with anybody but an eyewitness, or indeed Guðmundr himself. On the other hand, it might support Finnur Jónsson's dating as soon after 1202 as possible or Orri Vésteinsson's phrasing 'very shortly after 1200.'[1]

Finnur Jónsson must have thought that the date of composition soon after 1202 would account for the very foreshortened story of Guðmundr's life, which reaches only as far as his consecration; the supposition must be that the author simply knew of no later events. There is, however, evidence that the author knew of the later troubles, just as the author of *Páls saga byskups* knew about them, and simply suppressed them. He seems to have known that Guðmundr was something of a problematical character, and it is interesting to note

---

[1] Finnur Jónsson, *OOLH* (1920–1924), II, 569; Orri Vésteinsson, *The Christianisation of Iceland* (2000), 95.

that there is no eulogistic summation such as we find in *Hungrvaka*. At the beginning of chapter 4 he takes real umbrage at being 'beaten to book learning': 'He was very resistant, and it seemed clear in his conduct that he would take after his family in intransigence because he wanted to have the last word with anyone he dealt with.' Unlike his predecessors he is not a natural born scholar. Nor is he naturally religious. In chapter 7 he attends a church consecration in the West Fjords but takes no interest in it: 'Guðmundr thought it was more interesting to speak with the bishop's clerics than to attend services or the church consecration.'

The most palpable evidence that the author knew perfectly well about Guðmundr's troubled career is found in chapter 26 when he is served on a tattered tablecloth and dismisses an apology by saying: 'The cloth is of no concern. But my episcopacy may follow suit and be tattered like the cloth.' That is indeed the case, and we know from other versions of Guðmundr's saga just how tattered his episcopacy was. One version of the story follows in the wake of *Prestssaga* at the beginning of Sturla Þórðarson's *Íslendinga saga*.[1] It gives us, for example, more explicit information on the quarrel between Sigurðr Ormsson at Svínafell and Sæmundr Jónsson at Oddi. It turns out to be a quarrel over an inheritance, part of which Sigurðr has claimed, much to the distress of Sæmundr. The author of *Prestssaga* knows about this quarrel and assigns Sigurðr Ormsson a considerable role in his tale, but he does not tell about the outcome of the quarrel, in which Sæmundr emerges victorious while Sigurðr and his ally are discomfited. Kolbeinn nonetheless turns out to be the uncontested leader in the north, and in *Íslendinga saga* he is given full credit for appointing Guðmundr as bishop so that he can control both the secular and clerical contingents. The authority is more evenly shared in *Prestssaga*. Furthermore, the appointment of Sigurðr Ormsson and his wife Þuríðr (here identified as Kolbeinn's mother) is credited entirely to Kolbeinn, not to Guðmundr as in *Prestssaga*. We are told that Guðmundr and Sigurðr were on reasonable terms at first but soon fell out. The author of *Prestssaga* must have known this, but gives no hint of it.

Some ten pages of *Íslendinga saga* are then devoted to the contest between the newly consecrated bishop Guðmundr and the chieftain

---

[1] This long saga can be read in the translation of Julia H. McGrew in *Sturlunga saga* (1970), 117–447.

Kolbeinn Tumason.[1] The contention begins with disputes over court cases, and Guðmundr makes free use of excommunication, which Kolbeinn and his men just as freely ignore. The hostilities culminate in an armed confrontation in 1208, during which Kolbeinn is struck in the head by a rock cast by an unidentified assailant. The blow is fatal, and Kolbeinn dies on the field of battle. Eight of Kolbeinn's men also succumb, while the bishop loses only two men. Guðmundr nonetheless assesses heavy fines against his enemies, and his own men continue to rampage. In due course his opponents reorganise under new leadership and renew the attack, following up with executions and onerous fines. Guðmundr must be content to accept an invitation from Snorri Sturluson and escape to the west. He is never able to re-establish himself effectively. He tries to return to Hólar in 1218 but is forcibly removed.

Exactly how much of this later activity was familiar to the author of *Prestssaga* we do not know, but he surely knew some of the story. As we saw above, some scholars have nonetheless dated the composition quite early. There are, however, some general considerations that suggest a date later than the first decade of the thirteenth century. The saga is longer and more detailed than *Hungrvaka* or *Páls saga*. It is also livelier and more in line with what we might think of as saga style. Good examples of more dramatic storytelling can be found in the description of the shipwreck in chapter 6 and the confrontation between Guðmundr and Kolbeinn Tumason in chapters 26 and 27. In short, *Prestssaga* exemplifies a more advanced stage of saga writing than we find in the first bishops' sagas, including *Jóns saga helga* and *Þorláks saga*.

No matter how early *Prestssaga Guðmundar góða* was written, it seems clear that the outbreak of armed hostilities in 1208 must have been known to the author. He has nonetheless chosen to pass over the matter in complete silence. Such a radical concealment requires some explanation. It cannot very well proceed from ignorance but must be intended to make Guðmundr appear in a more favourable light. That is of course a regular feature of the bishops' sagas, none of which can be construed as a critique of the protagonist. Guðmundr, however, presented a particularly difficult case because everyone knew about the fierce resistance he had encountered in his see. The author therefore elected to optimise what people knew less about, namely his early years as a priest. This choice still confronts the author with

---

[1] *Sturlunga saga* (1946), 244–254; *Sturlunga saga* (1970), I, 134–345.

a difficult puzzle. He knew that in some ways his protagonist was a problematical character, but the rules governing his account required him to portray Guðmundr as an admirable figure. The task before him was to reconcile contradictory evidence. That makes his saga more challenging than the simple laudations we find in the earlier texts, where exceptional promise is followed by predictable fulfillment.

The author finds a solution for this quandary. He surmises that when Guðmundr was ordained (in March of 1185), his new status had a salvific effect just as, on a broader historical plane, the whole process of conversion, which is at the centre of the bishops' sagas, brought about a spiritual renewal in the population as a whole. Guðmundr's change of heart is described in chapter 11: 'The priest Guðmundr then became such a devoted man in prayer and holy services and openhandedness and self-mortification that it seemed to some people to border on excess.' He devotes himself to teaching and book learning, which had been anathema to him in his boyhood. His faith is judged to be at a level not previously aspired to in Iceland.

The author has not only a religious but also a psychological explanation for the change. He explains that it came about when Guðmundr was disabled in the shipwreck. After that, so we are told, 'every season saw some improvement in his character.' This is the first we have heard of such a character transformation, an idea that has not been properly forecast in the earlier part of the saga. It is nonetheless of considerable literary interest inasmuch as evolving character is not a phenomenon to any extent in the sagas generally. In both the kings' sagas and the sagas about early Icelanders a character is established at the outset and remains constant throughout. It seems clear that the Christian preoccupation with conversion and spiritual growth has paved the way for a new character dynamic. This dynamic did not find its way into the three previous sagas translated here and is a new feature in *Prestssaga Guðmundar saga góða*. That might reinforce the view that it represents a more advanced stage in saga writing and was composed somewhat later than the earliest bishops' sagas.[1]

Another indication of more advanced composition is the placement of the miracle stories. In the earlier bishops' sagas, such as *Jóns saga helga* and *Þorláks saga*, the miracles are narrated separately as a kind of supplement to the biographical story, but in *Guðmundar saga* they

---

[1] But cf. Anthony Faulkes, ed., *Two Icelandic Stories* [London], 1951, 15–16.

are integrated into the biographical narrative. It is significant first of all that there is no hint of miracles before Guðmundr's transformation in chapter 11, but they begin to appear in chapter 14 and persist in chapters 19, 20, 21, 26, and 29, always in conjunction with the biographical thread. Although the miracles are given ample coverage, there is not as much as we might wish about Guðmundr's daily routines. As in other bishops' sagas, there is some attempt to establish Guðmundr's secular credentials as well as his religious devotion. This balancing exercise is found in *Hungrvaka* and *Páls saga* as well; bishops were sometimes chieftains in addition to being clerics so that they had dual functions. Guðmundr Arason was not a chieftain by birthright, as the early chapters relate, although he seems to have acted the part once he became a bishop. His grandfather Þorvarðr is a chieftain, and in chapter 25 assumes a chieftainly tone in dealing with Guðmundr. He even allows for Guðmundr to become a chieftain in the future: 'Then the chieftainship will devolve on you after me.' Guðmundr's competence in secular matters is, however, open to question. Some effort is made to credit him with legal skills. At the beginning of chapter 8 he is put in charge of a case calling for outlawry, and the prosecution succeeds. A second lawsuit, growing out of the first, also comes to a successful conclusion in the following chapter, but that is largely due to the help afforded Guðmundr by Bishop Brandr and his son Þorgeirr. Guðmundr himself does not appear to have had further experience in the law.

Nor is he reputed to have had any skill as a businessman. In chapter 25 it appears in a conversation with Kolbeinn Tumason that there was a meeting at Víðivellir in Skagafjǫrðr in which the relative merits of Guðmundr and another candidate (Magnús Gizurarson) were discussed. Kolbeinn reports that 'there seemed to be more help and support from him [Magnús], and more financial experience in his case than yours.' It is indeed unclear how Guðmundr could have had any experience in this area because he did not fall heir to an inheritance and seems not to have owned any property. This lacuna in his qualifications must be remedied by issuing an invitation to Sigurðr Ormsson and his wife Þuríðr to act as managers and treasurers of the church estate. Their appointment is met with popular approval, but it leads to somewhat tense negotiations and, as we know from *Íslendinga saga*, a rapid deterioration in the relationship of Guðmundr and Sigurðr. It seems quite evident that there are shortcomings in Guðmundr's preparation to be bishop.

The author hints at the shortcomings but also seems to gloss over them. How exactly Guðmundr manages his life is quite obscure. He has no inheritance and no property, nor does he have a steady position, though Bishop Brandr offers him one in chapter 16. How then does he support himself? One of the recurring motifs is that he is regularly invited by people to stay with them for longer or shorter periods. He therefore seems to lead a sort of parasitic existence as an itinerant preacher, although no resentment is reported, and his hosts seem only too glad to have him. He even seems to have some money at his disposal because at one point in chapter 19 he makes a gift of thirty hundreds to finance the marriage of a relative. The source of his livelihood remains unexplained.

Also unexplained are the reasons for his popularity and prominence. He is admired and sought after both by the people at large and the leading figures in Iceland. In chapter 15 Guðmundr takes up residence at Vellir in Svarfaðardalr, but in the following chapter the abbess at Kirkjubœr invites him to come to her monastery in the capacity of a manager—apparently unaware of his inexperience in this area. Guðmundr is inclined to accept and prepares to leave, but his neighbours in Svarfaðardalr are so opposed to his departure that they appeal to Bishop Brandr and ask him to issue a prohibition. He duly complies, and Guðmundr is not allowed to move to a different quarter. Again, we are not told what Guðmundr has done to earn such exceptional good will, but he is retained in Svarfaðardalr by popular demand.

He is also singled out for special privileges, as is best exemplified in chapters 17–18. In the service conducted to honour Bishop Þorlákr's relics Guðmundr is allowed to sit with the two bishops Páll and Brandr and accompany the casket with Saint Þorlákr's remains. He is invited to visit Sigurðr Ormsson, who, as we have seen, was a prominent personality. He attends Snorri Sturluson's wedding feast at Hvammr and is treated with 'honour and affection' by Kolbeinn Tumason, who calls him a 'truly saintly man.' He is then invited by Bishop Brandr to take charge of the translation of Bishop Jón's relics, and the ceremony is delayed to await his arrival. When Saint Jón's feast day is adopted at the Alþingi the following year, it is Guðmundr who delivers the crucial speech. In chapter 19, when he visits the monastery at Þingeyrar, there is a special procession in his honour, and he delivers a lengthy sermon. In the following chapter Bishop

Páll Jónsson invites Guðmundr to perform the funerary dirge for the nun Ketilbjǫrg: 'That service was so notable that Gizurr [Hallsson] testified in his oration over her grave that they felt they had never heard such a funerary dirge, and he accounted her holy because such a performance was granted her.'

According to Bishop Páll, in a census reported in his saga (chapter 11), there were 190 priests in Iceland around 1200, and we may ask why Guðmundr is singled out for such singular deference, but the reason is once more unexplained. How many of the honours are factually true cannot be known, but his progress from relative obscurity to candidacy for bishop must in itself mean that Guðmundr had special capacities and a special presence. The author of *Hungrvaka* had a certain lexical richness to convey the personal qualities of his bishops, but the author of *Prestssaga Guðmundar góða* has no equivalent store of vocabulary and leaves us with nagging questions.

HUNGRVAKA (FORETASTE)

1. The Purpose of this Book

I entitle this booklet *Hungrvaka* (Foretaste) because many people, both learned and uninformed, who have looked through it, will want to know much more precisely about the origin and lives of the notable men about whom only a little is told in this account. Still I have recorded in writing practically everything that I have committed to memory. I have composed this booklet to prevent losing from memory that which I have heard about these matters from the learned man Gizurr Hallsson and what other notable men have put in story form.[1] This written account is also designed to inspire young men to familiarise themselves with and read our language, whatever is written in Norse laws or narratives or genealogy I have chosen to set this down in writing rather than other learned matters in written form because it seems to me that our children and other young people are most obligated to know or explore how and in what way Christianity came of age here and how the episcopal sees were established here in Iceland, and also to know what remarkable men those who have been bishops in this country have been. That is what I intend to relate.

I feel obliged to write about how the church was founded and developed in Skálaholt and the situation of those men who maintained it, since with God's grace I have been allotted all of this world's good fortune in their wake. But I

---

[1] Gizurr Hallsson was a chieftain and lawspeaker in southern Iceland. He died in 1206.

have the feeling that wise men may think that this booklet is like the material of a spoon made of horn because it is awkward to use when poorly made but very fair when it is perfected. People who are drawn to this booklet can make use of it to entertain themselves and others who wish to listen to it in all humility rather than using some other options that otherwise seem dull, for many have had the experience that, if they are looking for short-term amusement, it is followed by extended ruefulness. It seems to me to be the right solution that everyone should make use of this meagre information written down here as best suits him, if it holds his interest, and then retain that which is most pleasing and dismiss what does not appeal to him. It seems to me best that [the reader] should preferably revise what seems trivial here if he knows something closer to the truth rather than make sport of this and not be willing or not have the capacity to revise. I have compared this to a spoon made with horn because it seems to me to contain excellent material, but I know that it is much in need of improvement, and I will dedicate myself to that end as long as I am able to revise. I am also obliged to do so because it is no doubt my responsibility and negligence if there is anything in this matter that turns out to be wrong in its present form, and it is not the fault of the men from whom I believe I have taken this information. It is an old saying that a house should have residents. For that reason I will tell first how the residence was built at Skálaholt and further along about the individuals who maintained the church estate.

2. Bishop Ísleifr

Ketilbjǫrn the Old lived at Mosfell and had many children. One of Ketilbjǫrn's sons was named Teitr. He was such an auspicious man that he was the first to settle the residence called Skálaholt, which is now the most splendid residence in all of Iceland. Another aspect of his good fortune was that he had a son named Gizurr the White, who came to Skálaholt in the Christian era and lived at Skálaholt after his father Teitr. Gizurr the White was married to three women. First he was married to Halldóra, a daughter of Hrólfr from Geitland.[1] They had a daughter, Vilborg, who was married to Hjalti Skeggjason. Gizurr was then married to a woman from Eyjafjǫrðr named Þórdís. Their son was Ketill, who was married to Þorkatla, the daughter of Skapti. Gizurr was married last of all to Þórdís, the daughter of Þóroddr the Chieftain at Hjalli in Ǫlfus, and they had many children. They had a son named Ísleifr; Gizurr accompanied him abroad and entrusted him for the purpose of education to a certain abbess in a town called Herford.[2] Ísleifr returned to Iceland when he was a priest and well educated. He married and took to wife Dalla, daughter of Þorvaldr from Áss.[3] They had three sons. Gizurr was one of their sons, and he later became a bishop. Another was Teitr, who later lived in Haukadalr. A third was named Þorvaldr, who lived at Hraungerði and was a great chieftain. Gizurr the White built the first church at Skálaholt and was buried close to the church. Ísleifr lived at Skálaholt after his father. Ísleifr was a handsome man in appearance and generally popular; for all his days he was just and upright, generous and benevolent but never wealthy.

[1] Geitland is a correction of the MS reading *Gautland* and is identified as a property in Borgarfjǫrðr by Ásdís Egilsdóttir in *Biskupa sögur* II (2002), 6 n.1.
[2] Herford is a town in Nordrheinwestfalen (Germany), close to Bielefeld.
[3] Áss is a farm in Vatnsdalr south of Húnafjǫrðr in the north of Iceland.

When Ísleifr was fifty years of age and Christianity was not much older in Iceland, he was designated bishop by all the Icelanders and asked to go abroad. Then he departed and sailed south to Saxony. He paid a visit to Emperor Heinrich (1039–1056), the son of Konrad, and presented him with a polar bear from Greenland; that animal was a great treasure.[1] The pope sent a letter to Archbishop Adelbert of Bremen to the effect that he should consecrate Ísleifr as bishop on the Sunday of Pentecost. The pope said that with God's grace he expected the excellence of the episcopate to be most long-lasting if the first bishop to serve in Iceland were consecrated on the day when God adorned the whole world as a gift of the Holy Spirit. At the command of the pope Ísleifr was then consecrated as bishop on that day by Adelbert, archbishop of Bremen, fourteen days before the feast day of Columbanus (543–615). The archbishop provided all the appurtenances needed for the honour of a bishop according to the instructions of pope and emperor.

Then Bishop Ísleifr travelled that same summer to Iceland and established his episcopal see at Skálaholt. He had great trouble in many respects because of people's disobedience.[2] Indicative of the difficulties in which he found himself because of a lack of faith and disobedience and the depravity of those subject to him was that the lawspeaker lived with mother and daughter[3] and some men conducted viking activities and harrying. Men practised many other deplorable things that would now seem to be enormities if men committed them.

[1] On the traffic in polar bears in medieval Scandinavia see most recently Carla Cucina, *Auðun e l'orso* (2017), esp. 102–143.
[2] On the theme of popular disobedience see p. xii above.
[3] He presumably consorted with mother and daughter in succession, a case of forbidden incest.

In the days of Bishop Ísleifr bishops came to Iceland from other countries, and they practised greater leniency than Bishop Ísleifr.[1] As a result they became popular with wicked men until Archbishop Adelbert sent a letter to Iceland forbidding people to accept ministrations from them and saying that some were excommunicated and that all of them had come without leave.

In the days of Bishop Ísleifr a bishop named Kolr came to Iceland and died here. He was buried in Skálaholt, and this was the first church to be adorned with the burial of a high-ranking man. It is rightly called the spiritual mother of all the other consecrated buildings in Iceland.

Bishop Ísleifr always had tight funding for his household; there were few resources and a numerous attendance, and for that reason he was in strained cirumstances. Many people sent him their sons to be educated and they in turn became good clerics. Two of them became bishops: Kolr in Vík in eastern Norway and Bishop Jón [Ǫgmundarson] at Hólar (1106–1121).

When Ísleifr had been bishop for twenty-four years, he became ill during Mass at the Alþingi so seriously and so suddenly that he was forced to lay aside his clerical garb. The priest Guthormr Finnólfsson from Laugardalr, on the counsel of the bishop, continued the Mass where the bishop had left off and completed the Mass. Then the bishop was brought home to Skálaholt, and place was made for him in the church. People asked him for good advice both with respect to the selection of a bishop and other matters that they thought needed to be discussed. He advised that they should ask the priest Guthormr to go abroad, saying that he was best suited among their

---

[1] These bishops are identified in the following chapter.

countrymen and adding that it would be hard to get a bishop in Iceland if they did not commit themselves to be more accommodating toward a successor than they had been toward him.

During the last part of Bishop Ísleifr's life many things occurred in connection with him that demonstrated his goodness toward those who could appreciate it, for many people who were brought to him quite mad departed from him having been healed. He blessed beer with a bitter herb in it so that it was perfectly drinkable, and he occasioned many other similar things even though I do not itemise what he did. The wisest people thought them to be great miracles. Ísleifr was consecrated as bishop when he was fifty years of age. At that time Haraldr Sigurðarson was king of Norway.[1] Bishop Ísleifr died on Sunday in the church at Skálaholt at midday, three days before the feast day of the Selja people (July 8).[2] He had been bishop for twenty-four years and he was buried next to the interment site of Bishop Kolr. From the birth of Christ there had passed 1073 (*recte* 1080) years.[3]

3. Other Bishops in Iceland

It is reported that bishops came out to Iceland in the days of Bishop Ísleifr, but Friðrekr was the only one to come earlier and become the subject of stories. The following came out, with whom people are most familiar: Bishop Jón the Irishman, and some people claim that he subsequently

---

[1] King Haraldr Sigurðarson (harðráði) ruled Norway from 1046 to 1066 and fell in an expedition to England shortly before the Battle of Hastings.

[2] On the people of Selja see *The Saga of Bishop Páll* below, chapter 2, n. 2.

[3] This and a few other Icelandic texts (including *Páls saga*) use a dating system advocated by the eleventh-century scholar Gerlandus, who dated historical events seven years earlier than our current system.

went to Wendland and converted many people to God. He was later seized and beaten, with both hands and feet severed, and the head last of all. With these torments he found refuge in God.

The third bishop to come to Iceland was Bjarnvarðr Vilráðsson, who was called 'the bookish.' Some people say that he was from England and was in the following of Saint Óláfr and later travelled to Iceland on his advice. The fourth was Bishop Rúðólfr, who some people think was named Úlfr and came from a family in Rouen in England. He spent nineteen years in Iceland and lived at Bœr in Borgarfjǫrðr. The fifth to come to Iceland was Bishop Heinrekr, who spent two years in Iceland. The sixth was the Saxon bishop Bjarnvarðr, who was in the retinue of King Magnús the Good, son of Saint Óláfr. He later travelled to Iceland and was there for twenty years.[1] He had two residences in Vatnsdalr, at Giljá and Steinsstaðir.[2] He blessed many things of considerable note, churches and church bells, bridges and springs, fords and lakes, great rocks and small bells, and these things are thought to reveal his true distinction and goodness. Bjarnvarðr was in Iceland while King Haraldr Sigurðarson was in Norway because they were not on good terms. Later he went abroad into the service of King Haraldr's son. After that he travelled to Rome at the request of the king and made peace on behalf of the expired Haraldr. When

---

[1] King Magnús ruled from 1035 to 1047 and left behind a particularly glowing reputation.

[2] Vatnsdalr runs south from Húnafjǫrðr in the north. No Steinsstaðir has been identified, but Kristian Kålund guessed that it might be an error for Sveinsstaðir. See P. E. Kristian Kålund, *Bidrag til en historisk-topografisk beskrivelse af Island* (1879–1892), II, 32–33. Both Giljá and Sveinsstaðir may be located on the first map in vol. II. See also Ásdís Egilsdóttir, *Biskupa sögur* II, 12, n.3.

the bishop returned, the king made him bishop in Selja. Later he went to Bergen and died there. It is the view of everyone that he was the most distinguished of men.

In the days of Bishop Ísleifr many great events transpired. In Norway there was the fall of the king, Saint Óláfr. King Magnús the Good also died. He died in Denmark and his body was brought north to Trondheim.[1] They both died before Ísleifr became bishop. After he became bishop King Haraldr Sigurðarson fell in England, and a little later Harold Godwinson.[2] Then King Magnús, the son of King Haraldr Sigurðarson, died, and Sveinn Úlfsson, the king of Denmark, and Þorkell Eyjólfsson, Gellir Bǫlverksson, Þorsteinn Kuggason, Snorri the Chieftain, and other outstanding men.

4. Bishop Gizurr

Gizurr, the son of Bishop Ísleifr, was born at Skálaholt, but he was educated in Saxony and ordained as a priest at an early age. When he came out to Iceland, he married and took to wife Steinunn Þorgrímsdóttir, who had previously been married to Þórir Broddason. They first settled down at Hof in Vápnafjǫrðr. Gizurr was a tall man with a broad chest, bright-eyed and with prominent eyes, of noble appearance and a most benevolent man, strong and with a keen intelligence. Gizurr was fully accomplished in all those matters that become a man. He was a great seaman in the early part of his life, as long as Ísleifr was alive, and

---

[1] The return of King Magnús's body may be read in *Morkinskinna* I, 167–173, and *Morkinskinna* (trans.), 181–187; or in *Heimskringla* III, 105–106, and *Heimskringla* (trans.), III, 63.

[2] The fall of King Haraldr is related in *Morkinskinna* I, 310–321, and *Morkinskinna* (trans.), 181–187, or *Heimskringla* III, 186–192 and *Heimskringla* (trans.), III, 115.

was always much respected wherever he went and was associated with noble men when he was abroad. Haraldr Sigurðarson was then king in Norway and spoke words to Gizurr to the effect that he seemed to him most fit to bear any noble title allotted to him. He and his wife journeyed to Rome before settling in Iceland.

Gizurr was not in this country when his father died and arrived the following summer at the time of the Alþingi. He landed at Rangaróss and stayed on the ship for a few nights. He was unwilling to ride to the Alþingi as long as no one was elected bishop at the meeting. The chieftains asked the priest Guthormr to go abroad because they thought that this was what Bishop Ísleifr had chiefly in mind. It eventually came about that he consented to it if it seemed that no other option was available.

But when Gizurr learned that the priest Guthormr was ready to undertake the trip abroad, he rode to the Alþingi. When Gizurr arrived at the Alþingi, the priest Guthormr stepped onto the pavement in front of the church and announced to everyone that there was no chance of his going abroad now that Gizurr was available. Public opinion then turned to Gizurr, and they asked him to go abroad, but he made many excuses. But eventually it came about that he agreed to accept the difficulties, and all the chieftains promised him to be submissive to all of God's ordinances and do whatever he commanded if consecration fell to his lot. Then he set out that same summer. When he came to Saxony, Archbishop Liemar had been stripped of his office. He then went on to meet with Pope Gregory VII (1073–1085) and gave him a full account of his travels and the manifold difficulties involved. The pope then sent Gizurr to Archbishop Harðvík (Hartwig) of Magdeburg

(1079–1102) in Saxony and ordered that he consecrate him as bishop. Harðvík received him with great honour and distinction and consecrated him as bishop four days before the latter feast day of Saint Mary (September 8). He was then forty years of age, and the archbishop gave him readily everything that was needed.

After that Bishop Gizurr travelled out to Iceland, and all the people gave him a joyful reception. He gained great honour and respect from the very outset of his career as bishop, and everybody wished to do exactly as he ordered, young and old, rich and poor, women and men, and it was proper to say that he was both king and bishop over the country as long as he lived. He did not have all of his land as a domicile at Skálaholt for a time at the beginning of his episcopacy because his mother Dalla wished to live on her share of the land while she was still alive. But when she had died and the bishop had taken over all the land, he attached it to the church in Skálaholt that he himself had caused to be built, thirty ells in length, and dedicated to the apostle Peter. Bishop Gizurr bestowed many other endowments on this church, both in lands and ready resources, and he stipulated that this should always be the bishop's see as long as Iceland was inhabited and Christianity was maintained. Bishop Gizurr gave the church in Skálaholt a precious white cope, the best one for a long time thereafter, and many other treasures as well.

These men were contemporaries of Bishop Gizurr: the priest Sæmundr in Oddi, who was wise and the most learned of men;[1] the lawspeaker Markús Skeggjason, who was a great sage and a skald. They consulted together

---

[1] Sæmundr Sigfússon (1056–1133) had an imposing reputation. There is good evidence that he wrote a Latin history of the Norwegian kings, now lost.

and sought advice from the chieftains on passing a law that required people to pay a tithe on their property and all capital increase every year, as is customary in other countries inhabited by Christian people.[1] On the strength of their intelligence and wise urging the conclusion was reached that people agreed to the payment of a tithe that should be divided four ways, one part to the bishop, another to the churches, a third part to the clerical teachers, and a fourth part to the poor. There was no other provision for income or amenities at Skálaholt other than the tithe payments that were contributed because of the popularity and wisdom of Bishop Gizurr.

Steinunn Þorgrímsdóttir was in charge of the indoor household at Skálaholt while Bishop Gizurr attended to the see. That charge had fallen to Dalla when Bishop Ísleifr was still living.

When Bishop Gizurr had occupied the see for twenty years or so, the northern Icelanders made the request of him to have their own bishop and to establish a second see in the northern quarter, all at their own expense. There would thus be two episcopal sees in Iceland, and they expected that it would be seldom or never that the country would be without a bishop if there were two episcopates. Bishop Gizurr granted this request to the northerners with God's help, and subsequently the priest Jón Ǫgmundarson was chosen as bishop by God and good men. He travelled with letters from Bishop Gizurr and waited on Pope Paschal II. He was consecrated as bishop by Archbishop Ǫzurr at Lund in Scania two days before the feast day of Philip and James (May 1, 1101). Jón then travelled to

[1] In this paragraph the tithe is credited to Bishop Gizurr's wisdom, but for a more probing analysis of how the tithe was introduced see Orri Vésteinsson, *The Christianization of Iceland* (2000), 67–92.

Iceland and established his see at Hólar in Hjaltadalr in Skagafjǫrðr.

Bishop Gizurr had had the farm owners in Iceland counted, those who owed attendance at the Alþingi. There were 700 in the East Fjords, 1000 in the southern quarter, 900 in the western quarter, and in the northern quarter there were 1200, and that quarter was the wealthiest on average.

5. Continued

When Bishop Gizurr turned seventy-five, he became so unwell that he could not get out of bed and could not attend the Alþingi. He then sent word to his friends and all the chieftains at the Alþingi that the priest Þorlákr Runólfsson should be asked to go abroad. But the latter made excuses because of his youth and for many other reasons. But the matter concluded with his agreement to undertake the difficulty if that was the bishop's counsel. Then Bishop Gizurr had his journey prepared so that he was well equipped in every respect, and he gave him a letter to Archbishop Qzurr. But Bishop Gizurr's illness grew worse and became acute and painful and hard to bear, and his skin broke out in open sores down to the bone so that the pain caused great discomfort.

When it began to affect him severely and people thought they could hear the bones creak at the touch, his wife Steinunn went to his bed and asked how ill a man should be before one should make a vow for him. The bishop answered: 'The only thing that one should ask of God, if anything at all is to be asked, is that my discomfort should continue to increase as long as I can stand it, for there is no point,' he said, 'in trying to elude

God's struggle since the end of my life is at hand, though many things have gone well before.'

He was also asked where he wished to be buried, and he answered with compunction and great humility: 'Do not bury me anywhere near my father,' he said, 'for I am not worthy to rest close to him.'

Then he arranged everything as he wished it should be before he died. All his sons died before him except Bǫðvarr. His daughter Gróa survived him and was married to Ketill Þorsteinsson. Gizurr was consecrated as bishop when he was forty years of age. At that time Óláfr kyrri (1066–1093) was King of Norway, and he was the son of Haraldr Sigurðarson. Bishop Gizurr died on the third day of the week twelve days before Columbanus's feast day (June 9). At that time he had been bishop for thirty-five years. He was buried next to his father. There had passed since the birth of Christ eleven hundred and eleven years (*recte* 1118). Many people were so overwhelmed by Bishop Gizurr's death that they could not forget it as long as they lived. But it was the consensus of everyone that there would never be a replacement for him. It was also the view of all prudent men that, by dint of God's benevolence and his own achievements, he was the most distinguished man in Iceland, both among clerical and secular men.

In the year when Bishop Gizurr died the following also died: Pope Paschal II, Baldwin, king of Jerusalem, Arnulf, the patriarch in Jerusalem, Alexius Komnenus, emperor in Constantinople, and Philip I, King of France (died 1108). There was also a bad storm. There was such a tempest before Easter that the clerics could not hold services in the churches in the north on Good Friday, and a ship fetched up below Eyjafjǫll and turned over and landed upside down. Only a small number of people could take communion on Easter Sunday, and some perished. Another storm occurred when people were riding to the Alþingi, and it struck people's animals in the north. It also damaged the church at Þingvellir, for which King Haraldr Sigurðarson had provided the timber.

That summer thirty-five ships came to Iceland, but eight returned to Norway in the autumn after Michaelmas (September 29). That increased the population in Iceland so that there was a great increase in famine in many districts. The wisest of men thought that Iceland seemed to decline after the death of Bishop Gizurr just as Rome declined after the fall of Pope Gregory.[1] The loss of Bishop Gizurr pointed in the direction of all the decline in Iceland, both in shipping losses and the loss of life with the resulting loss of revenue, and beyond that hostility and lawlessness as well as mortality in the whole country such as had not occurred since the country was settled. Two years after the death of Bishop Gizurr Hafliði Másson was wounded at the Alþingi, and the case was not settled that summer.[2]

Bǫðvarr alone among the sons of Bishop Gizurr was still alive when he died, and his other sons, Teitr, Ásgeirr, Þórðr and Jón, had died previously. Gróa lived a long time afterward and became a nun and died at Skálaholt during the days of Bishop Klœngr.

---

[1] The reference must be to Pope Gregory I the Great (590–604), but I am unable to trace the idea that Rome declined after his death. It could conceivably be a vague reminiscence of the Langobardic invasion of Italy in 568 and the ensuing troubles.

[2] The story is told in *Þorgils saga ok Hafliða* from perhaps as early as the 1220s. It can be read in the translation of Julia H. McGrew in *Sturlunga saga* (trans.) II, 25–70.

During the episcopacy of Bishop Gizurr there were many significant events: the death of King Cnut (1086) on Fyn[1] and his brother Benedict as well, the death of the English king William [the Conqueror], the death of King Óláfr kyrri (1093) and Hákon the son of Magnús in Norway (1094), the fall of King Magnús Bareleg (1103) to the west in Ireland in Ulster, the translation of Bishop Nicholas the Saint to Bari (1087), the death of King Óláfr Magnússon in Norway (1115), the death of Saint Magnús, a jarl (1116), the death of the law-speakers Markús (1107) and Úlfheðinn (1116–1117) and of Teitr Ísleifsson (1110–1111) and the other sons of Bishop Ísleifr, the eruption of Heklufell (1104), and many other notable events even if they are not included here.

6. Bishop Þorlákr

Þorlákr was the son of Runólfr, the son of Þorlákr, the son of Þórarinn, the son of Þorkell skotakollr, and the son of Hallfríðr, Snorri's daughter, and Snorri was the son of Karlsefni. Þorlákr was raised at his father's home as a child, and he was educated at Haukadalr. He was intelligent at an early age, well behaved and well disposed toward all good people. He was much given to prayer at an early age, had a quick intelligence, and was fit for the priesthood. He was gentle and humble and unaggressive, helpful and benevolent to everyone around him, soft-spoken and compassionate toward those in need, close to his kin and restrained in all matters, both on behalf of himself and others. Þorlákr was forty-two years of age when he was

---

[1] This is the Danish king Knud den Hellige (Saint Cnut) who was killed by a rebellious faction in a church in Odense in 1086. He came to be reputed as a martyr and saint.

chosen as bishop, and it can be judged what kind of a man he was because the man who chose him for the most strenuous office was the wisest and most distinguished and best known to him, and that was Bishop Gizurr.

Þorlákr was of medium height, with a long face and light brown hair, amiable but not generally thought to be a handsome man or of deep intelligence in the eyes of most people. When he went abroad, the reaction was that there was not a great deal of choice in this country, and he seemed to them unqualified for such an honour. He himself answered that it did not amount to that and the cause was that he had more concealed his defects from men than from God.[1] On the basis of this response people thought that he would be well suited for the honour. When he went to meet Archbishop Ǫzurr, the latter quickly perceived who Þorlákr was and received him honourably and with respect, but he had some hesitation about consecrating him and said that he could not pile one head on top of another.[2]

But still, on the basis of Bishop Gizurr's request, he committed himself to consecration, though he did not wish to consecrate him to a location where there was already another bishop. He asked him to choose a [different] location for consecration but permitted him to be in Skálaholt if Bishop Gizurr consented to that, provided that he was still alive when Bishop Þorlákr returned to Iceland. Þorlákr was consecrated as bishop three days before the feast day of Philip and James (May 3), and he was consecrated for a church at Reykjaholt in Borgarfjǫrðr. He

---

[1] The sense seems to be that, although Þorlákr can hide his defects from men, he cannot hide them from God.

[2] As the next sentence indicates, Archbishop Ǫzurr does not wish to appoint two bishops to the same see.

was consecrated in Denmark thirty days before Bishop Gizurr died in Skálaholt.

Bishop Þorlákr travelled to Iceland that same summer he was consecrated and people gave him a joyful reception, as was appropriate. He maintained the same humility in his episcopacy that he had had before, and he enhanced his good qualities and abridged none of them as long as he lived. He took many men under his tutelage, and they later became good clerics. In many ways he contributed to the support of Christianity in Iceland.

When Bishop Þorlákr had occupied his see for three years in Skálaholt, Bishop Jón Ǫgmundarson died at Hólar, and in his place was chosen Ketill Þorsteinsson for the church. He travelled abroad south to Denmark and was consecrated as bishop ten days after Candlemas (February 2) and returned to Iceland the same summer. During his days Bishop Þorlákr cleared the way to establish and write the section of the law on Christianity with the oversight of the wisest men in this country and the guidance of Archbishop Ǫzurr; they were both in a supervisory role, both Bishop Þorlákr and Bishop Ketill. There were many other things that they established and ordered for the improvement of their countrymen during their time.

Bishop Þorlákr offered to foster a child of Hallr Teitsson in Haukadalr, and Hallr's son Gizurr went to Skálaholt. The bishop was as loving to him as if he were his own son, and he prophesied what later came to pass, namely that such an outstanding man could hardly be found in Iceland, as later proved to be true.

The same priest always served Þorlákr as long as he lived and was bishop. His name was Tjǫrvi, the son of Bǫðvarr, a very virtuous man, who had previously been attached to Bishop Gizurr. On this basis, and on the basis of other admirable qualities exhibited day to day, one could tell how even-tempered he was in goodness during his life. Every day he sang a third of the psalter slowly and intelligently, and in free hours he taught or read holy books or attended to the care of those who needed it and sought him out. He was never idle. He was generous to the needy but known by people in general to be tight-fisted, though he never withheld money for good causes when it was needed.

When Bishop Þorlákr was three years short of fifty, he became ill and was confined to the sleeping quarters where he was accustomed to sleep together with his clerical colleagues. When his illness began to worsen, he had the book entitled *Cura Pastoralis* read over him.[1] That book was made by Pope Gregory and relates exactly what characteristics a man should possess when charged with the governance of other men. People thought they could see that he was more reconciled to his death than before the book was read. He then prepared for his death in his own way, and the people in general did not know how the illness progressed until the very time of his death.

Þorlákr was consecrated bishop in the days of Pope Gelasius (1118–1119). At that time he was forty-three. Eysteinn (died 1157) and Sigurðr Jórsalafari (died 1155) were the kings in Norway. Þorlákr died the day before the feast day of Saint Brigid (February 1) and had been bishop for fifteen years. He was buried with the previous bishops. From the birth of Christ there had passed 1126 (*recte* 1133) years.

---

[1] This influential book by Pope Gregory I the Great may be read in the translation by Henry Davis, *St. Gregory the Great: Pastoral Care* (1978).

7. Continued

It happened in the north on the same day Bishop Þorlákr died that at that very hour a wise and distinguished priest named Árni, the son of Bjǫrn Karlsefnisson, was on the road. He heard a beautiful song from the heavens above, and the cantilena of Bishop Lambert was being sung:[1]

> Sic animam claris caelorum reddidit astris,
> [quam sacer angelicus deduxit ad aethera coetus.]

> Thus he rendered his soul to the clear stars,
> [which the sacred and angelic company drew up into the air.]

It was known and proven that there was nobody nearby. It seemed to many people that this event was a great wonder, and they did not forget it.

There is a great deal that is notable and positive to say about Bishop Þorlákr Runólfsson. The following events took place during his episcopacy: Bishop Jón the Saint died at Hólar (1121); King Eysteinn and Sigurðr Jórsalafari died; the priest Sæmundr the Wise died in the same spring (1133) when Bishop Þorlákr had died during the previous winter; there were the killings of Þorsteinn Hallvarðsson and Þórir Símunarson; the lawspeaker Bergþórr died; there was the legal dispute between Hafliði Másson and Þorgils Oddason, as well as their settlement. Many chieftains were unmanageable in their dealings with Bishop Þorlákr because of their disobedience, in some cases dishonest dealing and crime, but he controlled everything as best he could.

---

[1] Lambert was a seventh-century bishop in Maastricht. Ásdís Egilsdóttir (*Biskupa sögur* II, 27) notes the line that follows and refers us to the *Analecta Hymnica Medii Aevi,* ed. Clemens Blume and Guido M. Dreves (Leipzig: O. R. Reisland, 1897), vol. 26, 232.

8. Bishop Magnús

Magnús was the son of Einarr, the son of Magnús, the son of Þorsteinn, the son of Hallr af Síðu and Þuríðr the daughter of Gils, who was the son of Hafr, the son of Svertingr, the son of Hafr-Bjǫrn, the son of Molda-Gnúpr. Magnús grew up with his father Einarr and his stepmother Oddný, the daughter of the priest Magnús Þórðarson from Reykjaholt. They said he was the most beloved of all their children. Magnús was set to the task of studying and passed through all the orders before he became a priest. Magnús was a handsome man in appearance and rather tall, with fair eyes and sturdy limbs, kindly and agreeable and very imposing in his demeanour and courtesy. He was engaging and humble toward all, generous and steadfast in his disposition, competent, loyal, well informed and well spoken. He turned out to be well qualified both at home and away from home. He was always conciliatory toward people no matter how he was related to the case, and he did not hold back either with respect to words or material resources.

After Bishop Þorlákr had died the previous winter, Magnús was chosen as bishop the following summer. He intended to go abroad that summer but was driven back to Blǫnduóss and spent the winter in Skálaholt. He sailed back to Norway the next summer. During the summer when he made that journey Magnús Sigurðarson and Haraldr gilli fought a battle at Fyrileif and Haraldr fled south to Denmark.[1] The candidate for bishop Magnús also travelled

[1] Magnús Sigurðarson defeated Haraldr gilli Magnússon at Fyrileif (now Färlev in southern Sweden) in 1134. See *Morkinskinna* II, 155–156 and *Morkinskinna* (trans), 360–361 or *Heimskringla* III, 280–281 and *Heimskringla* (trans.), III, 172.

south to Denmark in the autumn and presented King Haraldr with gifts. They became very good friends. Magnús went to meet Archbishop Qzurr, who received him honourably and consecrated him as bishop on the feast day of the apostle Simon (October 28). The next winter Bishop Magnús was in Sarpsborg until King Haraldr returned home. Then he joined him, and the king gave him a gracious reception with the greatest honour and respect. He stayed with him until he returned to Iceland, and he received worthy gifts from the king, a goblet that weighed eight marks and from which a chalice was subsequently made, and many other gifts, for the king was generous and lavish toward his friends.

Bishop Magnús came out to Iceland at the time of the Alþingi and arrived in Eyjafjǫrðr. He rode to the Alþingi and people were at the court and could not agree on a particular case. Then a man came to the court and said that Bishop Magnús was riding to the Alþingi. People were so delighted at this report that everybody immediately departed. The bishop then went out onto the pavement in front of the church and told all the people assembled the news of what had happened in Norway while he was abroad. All the people much admired his fluency and intelligence. It soon became apparent what an outstanding man he was in his generosity and management both on his own behalf and the behalf of others, for as long as he was bishop he never spared funds to reconcile those who were at odds and he always added his own contribution to resolve their differences. For that reason there was no dispute among men while Magnús was bishop. He maintained the same humility as before, and for that reason he was more popular than anyone else and had accomplished many great things toward this end.

Bishop Magnús greatly expanded the church at Skálaholt and then consecrated it. He set the day of dedication on the feast day of the people at Selja. Previously it had been on the day of the Exaltation of the Cross in the spring (May 3) when Bishop Gizurr had consecrated it. Bishop Magnús had the church altars that he had brought with him draped, and they became great treasures. He also brought out the costly material that a priest's cope is made of and is called altar cloth. Bishop Magnús also supported the church property with many acquisitions that have been very beneficial for a long time, both for the church and for those who subsequently maintained it. He acquired for the church at Skálaholt Árnes and Sandártunga and almost all of the Vestmannaeyjar before he died. He intended to establish a monastery there, but he did not live long enough.

When Bishop Ketill had become a good seventy years old, he went to the Alþingi and commended himself to the prayers of the clerics at the gathering of priests. Bishop Magnús then invited him home to Skálaholt for the church dedication day and a marriage that was to take place there. That feast was so elaborate that there were few precedents in Iceland. A great deal of mead was mixed, and all the other provisions were provided in great plenty. Friday evening both went to bathe at Laugaráss after the evening meal. Something of extraordinary importance happened there. Bishop Ketill died, and people thought that it was a very significant event. Great sadness overcame many people at that gathering up to the time that the bishop had been prepared and was buried. But with the arrangements of Bishop Magnús and the excellent drink that people consumed there they recovered rather more quickly than might otherwise have been the case.

After that Bjǫrn Gilsson was chosen as bishop in Hólar and he travelled abroad with letters from Bishop Magnús to Archbishop Áskell, and Bjǫrn was consecrated as bishop the day after the Exaltation of the Cross in the spring (May 3) and he travelled back here that same summer and was bishop at Hólar for fifteen years.

When fifteen years had passed since the death of Bishop Þorlákr Runólfsson and Magnús had been bishop for fourteen years, a misfortune broke over Iceland with a cost of life not matched by other events. When Bishop Magnús had travelled to the West Fjords and was staying at Hítardalr at Michaelmas (September 29), the next day after the feast day fire broke out in the evening in the residence, and the bishop was not aware of it before he thought it risky to exit. It was as if he was reluctant to do both things, both flee the threat of death, which he saw approaching, and [be guilty of] having always prayed to almighty God to spare him the sort of death that seemed to him an extended torment. Bishop Magnús lost his life in the fire together with eighty-two others. The priest Tjǫrvi Bǫðvarsson, who had always served him during his episcopacy, died there. Seven other priests perished there, all of them distinguished.

The bodies of the bishop and Tjǫrvi were almost unscathed and were brought to Skálaholt. Prudent men were sent to Fljótshlíð, the priest Páll Sǫlvason from Reykjaholt and Guðmundr Koðránsson, to report these tidings to Hallr Teitsson and Eyjólfr Sæmundarson and other chieftains who attended his feast. They immediately proceeded to Skálaholt. The priest Guðmundr Brandsson and Snorri Svertingsson and several worthy men came from the west with the bodies of the bishop and Tjǫrvi, and they arrived at Skálaholt on the feast of Dionysius

(October 9). On Gereon's Day (October 10) the bodies were interred by the graves of the previous bishops. No occasion has caused greater misery than when people were doomed to part in such a way that practically everyone had to take leave of a dear friend in Hítardalr.

Bishop Magnús was consecrated as bishop by Archbishop Qzurr in the days of Pope Anacletus II (1130–1138) and King Haraldr gilli (1130–1136) and Magnús Sigurðarson (1130–1139), both kings of Norway. At that time he was a year older than thirty-five. He perished in the house fire at Hítardalr on a Friday, one night after Michaelmas (September 29). There had passed from the birth of Christ 1141 (*recte* 1148) years. He had been bishop for fourteen years. While Magnús was bishop, the king's housemates betrayed Haraldr gilli.[1] King Magnús Sigurðarson and Sigurðr slembidjákn (died 1139) also fell. The killing of Þórir Steinmóðsson took place (died 1136), and the following men died: Archbishop Qzurr (died 1137), the lawspeakers Hrafn Úlfheðinsson (died 1139) and Finnr [Hallsson] (died 1145), and King Henry I of England (died 1135). Many other things happened during his life that were highly significant.

After the death of Bishop Magnús and during the following summer it was necessary to choose someone as bishop. Hallr Teitsson travelled abroad and spoke the language everywhere as if he had been a native, wherever he went. Hallr died in Utrecht as they travelled back and was not consecrated as bishop. When the death of Hallr Teitsson was reported in Iceland and people realised that it would again be necessary to choose a bishop, it was

---

[1] The story of Haraldr gilli (1130–1136) and how he was tricked and killed by Sigurðr slembir and a group of defectors is told in *Morkinskinna* II, 177–178 and *Morkinskinna* (trans.), 371.

the choice of all those men who had a voice, under the guidance of Bishop Bjǫrn at Hólar, that people should choose the northerner named Klœngr, the son of Þorsteinn and Halldóra, the daughter of Eyjólfr.

9. Bishop Klœngr

Klœngr Þorsteinsson was a handsome man in appearance and of medium height, lively and with a good presence and very personable, a good writer and a very learned man. He was a good speaker and steady in personal relationships and a great skald. He had been in the following of Bishop Ketill and in many respects shared his good habits. Klœngr went abroad the same summer that he was chosen as bishop with letters from Bishop Bjǫrn to meet with Archbishop Áskell, who consecrated Klœngr as bishop twelve days after Saint Mary's feast day in the spring (April 6, 1152). Later the same summer he returned to Iceland. Gizurr Hallsson had come from Rome and Bari to the south and came with him so that people could welcome two of the most outstanding men in Iceland at the same time. Great beams of timber arrived on two ships. Bishop Klœngr had had them felled in Norway for the church he undertook to build in Skálaholt, a church that was elegant beyond any other building constructed in Iceland, both in terms of timber and design.

When the bishop had come to his see in Skálaholt, he quickly became so popular with the people that, after he had been in office for a short time, even those who had been against him loved him dearly. That was not at all strange because he was generous and open-handed toward his friends and liberal and outgoing in almsgiving to the poor. He was gentle and humble toward all, cheerful and witty and even-tempered toward his friends so that he was always looked to for help in whatever was needed as long as he oversaw the see. He had the work on the church begun right away after he had spent a year in the see. Other people found the outlay for the church construction so great at every season, both in timber provision and construction costs and associated manpower that it seemed to discriminating men that it was necessary to spend all the church revenue from tithes and other contributions. On the other hand, the domain required such great income at every season because of the large congregation and the cost of hospitality and other expenditures that it seemed that all the money that the church had was needed for the expenses. In the third place, Klœngr had defrayed such well-attended feasts and bestowed such large gifts of money on his friends, who were numerous and distinguished, that an enormous outlay of money was required. But almighty God, who is the source of all benefits, did not allow a shortage of anything that was needed both for the church construction and other expenditures that the bishop wished to maintain while he was alive.

These were the chief architects of the church at Skálaholt: Árni, who was regarded as the chief architect, and Bjǫrn the Skilful Þorvaldsson. Illugi Leifsson also shaped the beams. When the church was complete, Runólfr, the son of Bishop Ketill, composed this stanza:

> Sturdy is the structure
> That the strong leader built
> For comfort-granting Christ
> And commendable the plan.
> A benefit it was that Bjǫrn
> Bolstered the house of God.
> Peter acquired the awesome
> Work of Árni and Bjǫrn.

10. Continued

Bishop Klœngr was such a great man of law, if he was appealed to, that he was a great chieftain both by reason of wisdom and word-craft. He was also acquainted with the laws of the land. For that reason the chieftains were fully involved in the cases that the bishop participated in. Nor was there any resolution in important cases without Bishop Klœngr's being recruited for each one. His most reliable friends were the men most honoured in Iceland, Jón Loptsson and Gizurr Hallsson. Bishop Klœngr also exchanged gifts with the greatest leaders in other neighbouring countries and for this reason he became popular both abroad and at home.

When the church was completed in Skálaholt to the point where the bishop thought it ready for consecration, the bishop held a great and splendid feast for his friends. He invited Bishop Bjǫrn and Abbot Nicholas and many chieftains, and there was a great crowd of guests. Bishop Klœngr and Bjǫrn both consecrated the church in Skálaholt, one outside and the other inside, and they both dedicated it to the apostle Peter as it had been before, and Abbot Nicholas delivered the sermon. It was on the feast day of the martyr Vitus (June 15, 1158). After the services Bishop Klœngr invited all those who had been at the consecration to partake of dinner, those who thought it more needful, and that was again done more from munificence than surplus provision as always proves to be the case when it is left to many foolish men when one wise man can manage it quietly by himself. This was full proof of the matter because no fewer people partook of dinner than seven hundred, and the provisions were strained when it was over. The feast was quite splendid as all the people thought who had been invited. And all of the distinguished guests were sent home with great gifts.

Bishop Klœngr had the church that he had caused to be built at Skálaholt adorned to the greatest extent he could, to the point where it was fully decorated in every respect. He had a gold chalice set with gemstones and gave it to the church. He also had big books for church services written, much better than previous ones. It was his overall concern to teach aspiring priests, and he wrote and sang psalters and gave all necessary instructions. He was considerably more given to self-mortification than other bishops had been, also to vigils and fasts and plain attire. At night he often went out barefoot in snow and frost. When Bishop Klœngr had been a bishop for ten years, Bishop Bjǫrn died at Hólar two days after the feast day of Luke (October 18, 1162), when he had been bishop for fifteen years. The following summer the priest Brandr Sæmundarson was chosen, and he took letters abroad from Bishop Klœngr to meet with Archbishop Eysteinn. He was consecrated as bishop on the latter feast day of Saint Mary (September 8) and stayed in Bergen over the winter, as did Jón Loptsson. Later the following summer the bishop travelled out to Iceland and occupied the bishop's see at Hólar, to which his consecration assigned him.

11. Continued

Bishop Klœngr retained his honour and popularity into old age so that all the worthiest people respected him greatly. But when he began to grow old, poor health came over him, and first of all open sores developed on his legs from the cold and self-mortification and other discomforts he had suffered. When both age and ill health began to beset him, he dispatched letters to Archbishop Eysteinn and he asked that he be given permission to surrender his national duties as bishop and select someone else in his stead according to the precedent of Bishop Gizurr. Word came back from the archbishop that, with his permission, he should choose a bishop and send him abroad, but that he should maintain the church services and instruction as long as he was able even if he was not able to make visitations.

Bishop Klœngr went to the Alþingi and applied to the chieftains asking that a man be chosen as bishop. Everyone counselled that he should choose the one he wanted. He chose Þorlákr Þórhallsson, who then was the abbot in Þykkvabœr, and it was Bishop Klœngr's good fortune to choose that man to follow him, who is now verifiably a saint, and everyone is sure to know that no other man has previously proved to be that except for Bishop Þorlákr the Saint who was then chosen as bishop. But still Bishop Klœngr was in charge of the church that year. The administration was difficult because there were no donations to the church, but still the revenue did not diminish. Bishop Klœngr himself handed over the church administration and entrusted it to Abbot Þorlákr and those he chose to help him. The last year of Bishop Klœngr's life he scarcely left his bed and prepared for his death as every prudent man would in a long illness.

Klœngr was consecrated bishop in the days of Pope Eugenius III (1145–1153) by Archbishop Áskell and during the time of the Norwegian kings Eysteinn and Sigurðr. At that time he was fifty-seven years old and he had been bishop for twenty-four years. He died three days after the feast day of Matthew and that is his anniversary, but four days if it is not a leap year; that was a Saturday during the Ember Days in Lent. There had passed since the birth of Christ 1169 (*recte* 1176) years, and he was buried beside the previous bishops. Abbot Þorlákr stood over him, both over his grave and his deathbed, and it was a great good fortune that such a man should stand over him both living and dead because the blessed Bishop Þorlákr is now in the presence of God.

There were many great events during the time Klœngr was bishop, though I can only mention a few. There was the death of the sons of Gilli (Haraldr gilli Magnússon, 1130–1136), the Norwegian kings, first Sigurðr (1155) and later Eysteinn (1157), and last of all Ingi (1161), and the death of Archbishop Jón (1157) and the fall of Hákon herðibreiðr (1162), and the death of Bishop Bjǫrn at Hólar (1162). In the days of Bishop Klœngr Archbishop Thomas the Saint was martyred in England (1170), and during his life there occurred a second eruption of Hekla. There was also an earthquake in which lives were lost. The following Icelanders died while Bishop Klœngr was in office: Jón Sigmundarson (1164) and Abbot Hreinn (1169), Páll Þórðarson (1171), and Guðmundr Ketilsson, the priest, Bjarnheðinn Sigurðarson and his brother Beinir. There was the killing of Helgi Skaptason (1175), and Nicholaus Sigurðarson fell in Trondheim (1176). It appears to us that in many respects there has been no such excellent man as Bishop Klœngr in Iceland. We are inclined to believe that his magnificent qualities will be remembered as long as Iceland is peopled.

Now we have come to the story to be told about the blessed Bishop Þorlákr, and the present story is put together here to promote pleasure, as a narrative for good people akin to other stories that have been written down before. But however well the story of each of them speaks of him, there is no fairer account in every respect than there is of this precious friend of God, Bishop Þorlákr, of whom it may rightly be said that he is the shining beam and gemstone of saints both in this country and elsewhere in the world. He may truly be called the apostle of Iceland just as Saint Patrick is called the apostle of Ireland, for they accomplished the work of the apostles themselves in their teaching and patience with disobedient and wrong-minded men.[1]

---

[1] On this theme see note 2 on p. 6 above.

THE SAGA OF BISHOP PÁLL JÓNSSON

1. The Characterisation of Bishop Páll

Páll was the son of Jón, a very distinguished man, the son of Loptr, who was in turn the son of Sæmundr the Wise. Jón's mother was Þóra, the daughter of King Magnús Bareleg, and Páll's mother was Ragnheiðr, the daughter of Þórhallr, sister of Bishop Þorlákr the Saint. Páll grew up in Oddi with his father Jón, who himself, along with others, attached greater and greater importance to him the older he got.

Páll was handsome in appearance, with bright, steady eyes and fair, curly hair, well proportioned and with small feet, with a fair and clear complexion, a man of medium build and a very mannerly man. He had an agile mind and was quick to learn at an early age, handy in everything he did, both in writing and everything else. He married at a young age and took to wife Herdís, the daughter of Ketill, a fair woman and accomplished in all matters that are a credit to women.

When they had been together for a few years, Páll went abroad and was attached to Jarl Haraldr in Orkney,[1] who held him in high esteem. Then he went south to England and studied there and became so well educated that it was almost unexampled that any man should acquire so much learning in such a short time. When he came back to Iceland, he outdid everyone else in his accomplishments

---

[1] Haraldr was a remarkably successful jarl in Orkney. His story is told in the last hundred pages of *Orkneyinga saga*. Born *c.* 1134, he was very early involved in the power struggles that prevailed in his region, but he was a survivor. *Orkneyinga saga* (*ÍF* 34, 297) tells us that he had the title of jarl for 48 years, the first 20 with Rǫgnvaldr jarl and the next 28 years on his own. He was eventually obliged to submit to King Sverrir, but he did not die until 1206.

in learning, his command of verse,[1] and his knowledge of book learning. He also had such a good voice and was such a good singer that his voice and performance exceeded all others who were his contemporaries. He then took up his residence in Oddi and was well treated, as was appropriate.

A little later Páll settled in Skarð,[2] and at first much that was needful was missing. But the skills of both spouses and the good will of their friends were to such good effect that in a short time they had whatever was needed. They then became the victims of a great economic shortfall, but they bore it admirably well. It was as if nothing had happened, and then their property grew like the sea washing onto the shore. Páll was solid and reserved and accommodating with all his friends and all men of good will, but he was tough with wicked men, thieves and scoundrels. He was much involved in all governance matters in his district and was right at hand when his presence was needed. Páll was a chieftain and supported all his followers in all proper matters so well they never suffered loss. Páll and his wife Herdís had four children who survived infancy, two sons and two daughters. His sons were named Loptr and Ketill and his daughters Halla and Þóra. All the children were good-looking and accomplished when they grew up.

Bishop Þorlákr, Páll's uncle, held him in high regard and loved him greatly, inviting him often. Though certain chieftains stood in opposition to Bishop Þorlákr, Páll was all the more a reliable kinsman and confidant the more others kept their distance. When Bishop Þorlákr died, Páll demonstrated a more loving attachment than almost all of his prominent friends.

---

[1] Learning to write Latin hexameters was a regular part of medieval schooling.
[2] Skarð is a farmstead a little to the northeast of Oddi.

2. Páll Elected Bishop

The summer after the death of Bishop Þorlákr the Saint, Páll was elected bishop. Beforehand there was an extended discussion about the matter, but eventually it was left up to Bishop Brandr, chiefly at the behest of Hallr Gizurarson,[1] and he chose Páll for the voyage abroad. Páll was not easily persuaded, and one after the other they undertook to urge him, Bishop Brandr as well as his brothers and other close friends, but he declined, and with that he journeyed home from the Alþingi.

Then he returned to Oddi on the day of the church's dedication, the celebration of the martyrs from Selja[2] (July 8, 1194), and he was in a great state of despondency. When everyone had given up urging him and there was nothing else to contend with other than God's will, and with that [resistance] being contrary to his wishes, and as he considered his situation, the Holy Spirit inclined him to make himself responsible for the needs of the people, so that he bravely took up the burden that his mind had long been urging on him. Not long after he went to Skálaholt together with his father Jón and his brothers and took in safekeeping all the church finances. He asked right away that Gizurr Hallsson stay in place because he had been there in the days of Bishop Þorlákr the Saint, a great ornament of the church and a resident gift to the people. Páll left all the finances in question in place at Skálaholt as they had been before, and he tasked the priest Þorkell

---

[1] Hallr Gizurarson is presumably a transposed form of the name as later references to Gizurr Hallsson suggest.

[2] The story of the martyrs on Selja is told in the 'Acta Sanctorum in Selio' in *MHN* (1880; rpt. 1973, 145–159). A group of holy refugees escape an attack by the pagan Jarl Hákon (975–995) because they are buried in the collapse of the caves in which they are hiding.

Hallsson with the maintenance of the church, a priest in his employ since his arrival. He was later a canon in Ver.[1]

Herdís maintained their farm at Skarð, as well as their children and possessions, properly and in good order during the time he was abroad. Common opinion held that no children had been so well brought up as theirs in the whole district. That remained the case for as long as she lived, for she was the most exacting of women both with respect to herself and others, as often proved true.

3. The Voyage of Páll as Bishop-elect

Páll went abroad the same summer he was nominated as bishop, and he was a deacon in orders at the time. His voyage went smoothly all the way to Norway, and he proceeded to the town of Niðaróss, where he spent the period until after Christmas. Whoever honoured him most was credited with the most proper conduct, all the more so the higher their standing, and they indeed judged correctly.

Archbishop Eiríkr was in Denmark when Páll went abroad for consecration, and he was with Archbishop Absalon. King Sverrir the Great was east in Vík and travelled from there to Upplǫnd. After Christmas Páll proceeded from the north, from the town [of Niðaróss], to meet the king and his train, for a multitude of royal followers were with him. The king received him as if it were his son or brother visiting him. He accorded him such honour and distinction as he himself or his friends might have chosen. It was a fact that he was more adroit than anyone else, and more able, and he turned everything to positive advantage that might distinguish them both.

---

[1] Ver housed a chapter of canons in the close vicinity of Þykkvabœr in southeastern Iceland.

4. Páll Consecrated as Bishop

Bishop Þórir ordained Páll as a priest in Hamarr. That was one night during the Ember Days in Lent after the feast day of Saint Matthew (February 25, 1195). Then he returned to the king the same night and stayed with him until he went to Denmark. The king gave him everything that he might need abroad. The king also had all the bishops in the country give him sealed letters. Then he went to Denmark during Lent and arrived at Lund the first day of Easter to meet the archbishop, and Absalon invited him as soon as he arrived and accorded him the greatest honour. He waited for him at High Mass as soon as he knew that he was to be expected. Then he stayed with the archbishops during Easter and enjoyed the most honourable reception from them both. His consecration was arranged forthwith because they quickly realised what a distinguished man he was both in learning and wisdom and in action. He awaited consecration in the monastery called Herrevad,[1] and he was consecrated sooner than expected when they parted, the main cause being that King Cnut Valdemarsson expressed himself to the effect that his journey should be scheduled to the best advantage of him [Páll] and his people, those under his episcopal authority. That was in accord with his other good fortune, to wit that the most exalted man valued him so highly, sight unseen, that he advised the very thing that he [Páll] himself would have chosen.

Archbishop Absalon consecrated Páll as bishop on the day of Bishop Jón [Qgmundarson—bishop at Hólar 1106–1121] eight days before the feast day of Philip and

---

[1] Herrevad was the oldest Cistercian monastery in Denmark (now Skåne/Scania) and was founded in 1144.

James (April 23, 1195) on the counsel of Archbishop Eiríkr, who himself could not see clearly enough to consecrate him. Present at the consecration of Bishop Páll were Archbishop Eiríkr and Bishop Pétr of Roskilde. Bishop Páll presented a gold ring to Archbishop Eiríkr, and he gave valuable items to all the others who endorsed his office and honour. Celestine was the pope at the time when Bishop Páll was consecrated.

Bishop Páll was forty years of age when he was consecrated bishop. Then he travelled to Norway and came together with King Sverrir in Vík out east and went with him to Bergen and stayed with him until he went out to Iceland that same summer. The king honoured him in every respect the longer he was with him and the better he got to know him. All held him in high regard, as was to be expected, and his kinsmen were the most distinguished men in the country.

5. Bishop Páll Assumed his Bishop's Seat in Skálaholt

Páll went to Iceland the same summer he had been consecrated bishop. He arrived in Eyjafjǫrðr and right away held a magnificent feast for Bishop Brandr and other friends who were on hand; there was wine to drink and all the best dishes in great number. It became apparent from the very outset, as was later confirmed, that he was always most content when he was delighting the largest number of friends and intimates at fine feasts with affection and outstanding attentiveness. He had brought with him two glass windows to present to the church in Skálaholt, his spiritual betrothed, and he promptly demonstrated, as emerged ever more clearly, how he planned and ardently wished to adorn the church still more than before after he was consecrated, even though it was already more finely and splendidly adorned than any other church in Iceland.

The first honour that Bishop Páll accorded his see and church beyond anything any bishop had done before was to celebrate no Mass before coming to Skálaholt. In all countries no less honour is attached to hearing the Mass of a newly ordained priest than to hearing a bishop's Mass, and this was all the more true because it meant hearing a priest's Mass and a bishop's Mass all at once. A great multitude gathered in Skálaholt on hearing the glad news in order to witness the first Mass of Bishop Páll. Many distinguished men were on hand: his father Jón Loptsson, his brothers Sæmundr and Ormr, Gizurr Hallsson, and altogether there was a great crowd. The bishop spoke at length and handsomely and, to everyone's delight, committed himself to maintain all the ordinances that Bishop Þorlákr had presided over. When he took over the office, it could easily be seen how kind and well-disposed he was toward all his staff and how unpretentiously he treated all those who were of service and performed tasks according to his dignity. In the process he became so popular among all that everyone, almost everywhere in the country, was heartily devoted to him both in his own diocese and elsewhere. It was also clear how good a financial administrator he would be in light of his attentiveness and consistent intelligence.

Bishop Páll had been in Skálaholt for a year before his wife Herdís came there to preside over the housekeeping, and she was such a helpmeet and support, both to the church and to him personally, that no one else matched her as long as he was in office. Her intelligence and management skills were so great that it did not take many years before everything that was needed was in good supply and no requests needed to be made for the farm, even though a hundred people were in residence in addition to seventy or eighty workers.

6. Concerning the Bell Tower Work at Skálaholt

When he arrived at his see in Skálaholt, Bishop Páll soon realised that it seemed proper to him to support and renew and finally complete what Bishop Þorlákr the Saint had intended and provided for, that is, to install the bells he had purchased for the church in Skálaholt and were the best in all Iceland. He had also procured from Norway four beams together with the bells, and they were twenty ells in length.

Bishop Páll also arranged with the man most skilled in carpentry in all Iceland, a man named Ámundi Árnason, to build a tower so outstanding in material and design that it supported no less weight than all the wooden structures in Iceland, including the church itself. He commissioned a church high up in the tower and a stairway up to it, and he dedicated the church to Bishop Þorlákr the Saint, on the tenth day of Christmas; he adorned the church beautifully in every respect and provided everything that was needed. He arranged for the priest Atli, a book illuminator, to paint the whole ceiling inside the tower, and the gable as well, and fit the lower area with three wall hangings in good and decorative fashion. He also had inscribed the date of interment on each burial marker belonging to those who lie in the tower. For the building of the tower structure he spent no smaller amount, by his own account, than four hundred hundreds or more. He bought the bells in the tower from a Norwegian named Kolr, and they were an outstanding treasure in their measurements. He bought even more bells for the tower and two matching bells over the church, and he adorned in every conceivable way both church and tower in their outward appearance with pictures and crosses, tablets, paintings, lamps and glass windows, and episcopal adornments of all kinds. He had a stone coffin carved with outstanding skill, in which he was laid after his death, and he had proper graves dug in the tower for the people to whom he thought he was most beholden.

7. The Sanctity of Bishop Þorlákr Came to Light

In the third year of Bishop Páll's episcopacy his father Jón Loptsson died on All Saints' Day (November 1, 1197), the man who was the most outstanding chieftain in all Iceland. He [Páll] counted it to be the greatest grief when that man was lost, the man who could most greatly exalt and strengthen his standing and was more committed to do so than anyone else.

But almighty God, who caused his good fortune and luck to grow constantly from day to day and never decline, so enhanced his honour that no man before him among his kinsmen in Iceland had become so outstanding and respected because of his close relative Bishop Þorlákr the Saint, whose glory and saintliness almighty God revealed first in the northern region and after that over all Iceland and other nearby countries. Although Bishop Páll was more cheered by this revelation than others, he proceeded so cautiously in this matter that he sided with all the chieftains and the wisest men on this claim and the conduct of the matter. It went to the point that the rumour was not dismissed among some people that he did not want to encourage the idea of blessed Bishop

Þorlákr's sanctity. He was motivated by the wish to repay God for the glory He brought to pass during his lifetime, such as had never occurred before, and he wanted to adhere to the process that might be expected to be most pleasing to God. It seemed to him problematical, as indeed it was, that a reasonable measure be far exceeded at the outset and stand in the way of the truth. But no one believed earlier or more fully in the glory and saintliness of blessed Bishop Þorlákr than he did, though he proceeded more cautiously than others. But all the wisest men concurred with Bishop Brandr's message that Bishop Þorlákr's holy relics be unearthed that same summer, as he himself instructed in a transparent vision that had come to the priest Þorvaldr the preceding Christmas.

After the Alþingi meeting that same summer, when this was decided, Bishop Páll sent word to Bishop Brandr and his brothers Sæmundr and Ormr, and the sons of Gizurr Hallsson, Þorvaldr and Magnús, and to Þorlákr's son Þorleifr in Hítardalr (the uncle of Herdís Ketilsdóttir), and to Þorlákr Ketilsson (Herdís's brother), and to the priest Guðmundr Arason, who later became bishop at Hólar, and to many other dear friends. Bishop Páll hosted a splendid feast for these men when assembled, and the holy relics of blessed Bishop Þorlákr were then unearthed and properly prepared according to the supervision and direction of Bishop Páll. Great miracles quickly followed, as is told in his saga, and that redounded to his glory and to the good fortune of Bishop Páll.

8. Concerning Vows and Coffin Manufacture

The following summer (1199) the feast day of Bishop Þorlákr was incorporated into the law throughout the land, and fasting for two days was instituted. After that people assembled from all over the country to worship blessed Bishop Þorlákr with night vigils and fasting, prayer and donations. People who were on the road also came, great crowds in both seasons, both people from abroad and Icelanders, fulfilling the vows they had made; they confided to Bishop Páll what they had vowed and the outcome of their vows and the miracles that had occurred in response, and these were always his delight. They took with them true confirmations of the saintliness and glorification of blessed Bishop Þorlákr and the magnificence and generosity of Bishop Páll.

Though great honour had already been accorded Bishop Páll, as was proper, even before the saintliness of Bishop Þorlákr was revealed, it redounded much to his credit that he had a truly outstanding maternal uncle, and many people considered that the old saying was borne out stating that men most resemble their maternal uncles. It seemed most likely that such was the case because he regularly followed in the footsteps of blessed Bishop Þorlákr. He was precise and observant in performing services. He was ascetic in fasting and dress. He was mindful of all those matters that he knew were the ways of blessed Þorlákr, humility and almsgiving, asceticism and patience, all of which were much tested in his episcopacy.

When it seemed to Bishop Páll that some resources had accrued from what people gave for the goodness of blessed Bishop Þorlákr, he soon showed what he had in mind. He then contracted with a goldsmith who was named Þorsteinn and was the most skilled metalworker in all of Iceland. Such was his provision that there was no shortage of what was needed for the project that he wished to arrange. He ordered the manufacture of a coffin and allocated a very large amount of money in gold and gems and refined silver. With contributions from others he allocated no less money for the coffin and the manufacture of it than four hundred hundreds. The manufacture was very elaborate and it was superior to any other coffin in Iceland in beauty and size, being three ells in length, while none other of the ones in Iceland was more than one ell. No intelligent man inspecting the coffin will inquire what great man it was who had the treasure made or for whom it was constructed with such precious material.

9. Concerning Jón, Bishop of the Greenlanders

In the days of Bishop Páll, Bishop Jón came from abroad in Greenland and wintered in the East Fjords. Toward the end of Lent he came to Skálaholt to meet with Bishop Páll, and he arrived on Holy Thursday (April 3, 1203). They both consecrated a provision of chrism and exchanged many devout words and wise remarks. Bishop Páll received him with the greatest honour and entertained him in worthy style during his stay. He bade him farewell with signal generosity both in material gifts and other honours. Bishop Jón advised people on how to make wine from crowberries [*empetrum nigrum*] as King Sverrir had instructed him. But it happened that during the following summer (1203) almost no berries grew in Iceland. But a man named Eiríkr, who lived a short distance from Skálaholt at a farm called Snorrastaðir, concocted some wine that summer and all went well. Bishop Jón travelled to Norway and then to Rome, and wherever he went he spoke of Bishop Páll's magnificence and noble bearing.

In the days of Bishop Páll, when Gizurr Hallsson was the lawspeaker, deception was widespread with respect to measurements, both among foreigners and Icelanders, to the extent that people thought it was no longer tolerable. Bishop Páll advised that people should have rods two ells in length. Others strongly agreed and supported that measure. Other chieftains reinforced the bishop on this matter, Gizurr and his sons Þorvaldr and Hallr and Magnús, and also the brothers of the bishop, Sæmundr, who was the most distinguished man in all Iceland, and Ormr, who was both learned in the law and wise in all matters, and all the chieftains as well. Law was established accordingly and has been maintained ever since.

10. The Episcopal Succession at Hólar

In the seventh year of Bishop Páll's episcopacy Archbishop Absalon died in Denmark on Saint Benedict's Day (March 21, 1201). In the same year Bishop Brandr died on Sixtus's Day (August 6) when he had been bishop for thirty-eight years and a great sage.

After the death of Bishop Brandr the northerners nominated the priest Guðmundr Arason as bishop, and Bishop Páll provided him with letters to submit to Archbishop Eiríkr. Guðmundr was consecrated bishop in Trondheim ten days before the feast day of Bishop Jón [Ǫgmundarson: bishop at Hólar 1106–1121] (April 13, 1201). At that time Hákon was King of Norway, the son of King Sverrir.[1] Bishop Guðmundr sailed to Iceland that same summer and arrived in the East Fjords. He and Bishop Páll met together and paid each other great honour in feasting and material gifts. Then Bishop Guðmundr proceeded to Hólar and occupied his see,

---

[1] Hákon, the son of King Sverrir, reigned briefly from 1202 to 1204.

and suffered great distress for many reasons. The income soon dwindled and the expenditures hardly seemed moderate. The people around him considered him rather harsh and stern in his commands. Bishop Páll became all the more popular and beloved by the people at large when they saw his attentiveness and the ease of his presence and oversight with respect to everyone under his sway. All the people of the country wished for such leadership if it was to be had.

11. Bishop Páll's Census of Churches and Priests

Bishop Páll conducted a census of the churches in need of priests in the three quarters under his oversight. He counted the number of churches needed in his district and that amounted to two hundred and twenty, for which one hundred and ninety priests were needed.[1] The reason he counted them was that he wished to allow priests to go abroad if there was a sufficient number left in his district, and he also wished to arrange that there should be no shortage of priests in his district as long as he was bishop.

12. Concerning the Life and Children of Bishop Páll

In the twelfth year of Bishop Páll's episcopacy important events came to pass. Gizurr Hallsson died two days before the feast day of Saint Óláfr (July 27, 1206). Bishop Páll's brother Sæmundr spoke about him with words to the effect that he was the centrepiece of joy wherever he was. Fire erupted from Mount Hekla for the third time three nights before the feast of Saint Ambrose (December 4, 1201) the following winter.

---

[1] Sveinbjörn Rafnsson (1993, 90–117) has made a close study of the surviving remnants of this inventory.

Bishop Páll was such a fortunate man that everything turned to his advantage in the early part of his life and he was acknowledged, as may be seen at the high point of this tale, in which I have departed very little from what happened, as being outstandingly good to everyone. Almighty God favoured him more as time passed both in wealth and honour. And if there are those who believe that I have exaggerated the story of Bishop Páll's life because of partiality more than is justified, they are not correct, for I have been more inclined to omit and pass over remarkable matters from his story on the grounds of my ignorance and inattention rather than misstate anything in my story.

Good fortune followed Bishop Páll even when people were beset by famine and the stock for winter was curtailed causing a shortage of provisions first for the animals and then for the people. Then he chose, with the concurrence of Þorvaldr Gizurarson and other wise men in his district, to call on God and the saints for relief by singing Pater Noster every day to honour God in memory of Bishop Þorlákr, and on his day in the summer to give [the poor] sheep's milk at the morning meal and a bundle of hay from each cow's manger and a measure of meal, and famine never recurred during his lifetime.

But God does not always wish to test his worshippers with favour alone but rather wishes to exalt them with temptation and exertion to see if they remain firm, as He has often demonstrated. When Bishop Páll's situation shone forth in the greatest prosperity and his honour and status continued to grow, Herdís secured all those things that the estate needed with her intelligence and supervision and all necessary activity in such a way that she was the most precise in every function among all those who were there on this estate and all the other properties that the bishop owned. Their children became accomplished at a young age, Loptr in skill and learning and wisdom, Ketill in judgment and handwriting, Halla in handiwork and book learning, Þóra in accommodation and affection. And because the Gospel says that all matters should be witnessed by two or three [Matthew 18.16; John 8.17], I adduce the testimony of Ámundi the Smith, who was both reliable and accurate. He composed this stanza:

> God favours Loptr's fortunes,
> He falters very little.
> Mighty Lord of the moon
> Magnifies Ketill's lot.
> The highest Lord lends you
> An excellent life, Halla.
> May the precious Presider
> On high promote Þóra.

Thus their fortunes prospered as long as they were unafflicted.

13. The Drowning of Herdís and Halla

When Bishop Páll had presided for twelve years in Skálaholt, it happened that Herdís left home in the spring after Easter for the farm at Skarð, which she and the bishop owned, in search of workers and to attend to other needful matters. Two of her children went with her, Ketill and Halla, but Loptr and Þóra stayed at home with the bishop. When Herdís was in Skarð there was a great downpour, and it made the river Þjórsá impassable. But she wished to return home on the specified day because there was a lot left to do at home awaiting her return. She located a boat to bring to the river, and the following people proceeded to the boat: Herdís, Ketill, Halla, Herdís's brother Jón, a priest named Bjǫrn (the bishop's chaplain, who was in their company), a deacon from Skarð named Þorsteinn, and Guðrún, who was the daughter of Þóroddr and Herdís's niece.

Ketill and Bjǫrn were the first to cross with their horses and riding gear. Herdís's horse was lost. The last time they were to cross, the priest Sigfúss Grímsson, the deacon Þorsteinn, Herdís, Halla and Guðrún were on board and the weather was rather stormy. When they got into the current and it was a short distance to the shore that they were supposed to reach, it happened that the boat capsized beneath them. They all went underwater but all surfaced again. Mother and daughter were audible as they sang and commended themselves and their souls to almighty God. Those destined to die and those destined to survive were separated. Sigfúss washed ashore, but Herdís, Halla, and Guðrún drowned, and the deacon Þorsteinn too, and Sigfúss was much overcome when he got to shore, and there was nobody on the shore with the fortitude to help. But almighty God fulfilled all his vows, having promised that he would give consolation for every grief and would test no one beyond endurance (1 Corinthians 10.13). God showed in this grievous event that consolation would quickly follow sorrow, and it came to pass that all the bodies of the people who had perished there were found the same day, and that was a great comfort, especially to the survivors. It was little to be expected unless God in his kindness and mercy granted it, because the water was so high that a few days later the lost horse washed up on the Vestmannaeyjar.

When this news was brought unexpectedly to Bishop Páll in the dead of night, it seemed to everyone that God had reckoned very narrowly what he could bear. He could take no food and could not sleep before the bodies were interred, but still he tried to keep everyone's spirits up to the extent he could. Still, anyone could imagine what suffering he endured in sorely losing the person he loved most and watching his children in constant sorrow along with all those he had in his care. He proceeded quietly with his observances of his loss both with gifts to the clergy and poor people, and he understood fully that it matters greatly and is better that a plough cut deep rather than on the surface.[1]

The day that was marked when Herdís and the others lost their lives with her was fourteen days after the Exaltation of the Cross (May 17, 1207) in the spring. It was the custom of many people, both laymen and clerics, to remember her as earnestly and lovingly as their nearest relatives because of her manifold solicitude. Bishop Páll lavished great comfort both in words and material gifts on Herdís's brother Þorlákr, and he honoured him in all respects no less than before he lost her. After her death he comforted Þorlákr no less than his own family. Þóra, the bishop's daughter, took charge of the house after her mother's death with the loving support of her father. At that time she was no more than fourteen years old, but she managed so well that those who were best acquainted with her admired her ways most of all. The bishop overcame his grief so soon, given what he had suffered, that most people paid little notice. But everyone may find it more likely that his patience was the explanation, and his wish to honour people with his kindness, rather than that his sorrow diminished as long as he lived.

[1] This turn of phrase seems to mean that important matters should be dealt with seriously and not superficially.

14. Concerning Bishop Páll's Assistants

Compared to earlier times, Bishop Páll rarely preached unless it was a special day, and he considered that it would be of greater import for everyone if it did not happen often. But almost every holiday he sang two Masses. Four days in every twelve-month period he preached a sermon himself: the first day of Christmas, the Wednesday of Lent, Holy Thursday, and the day of the church's dedication. Other days he preached only when it seemed that there was some compelling reason. I take note of such matters because even the most meticulous and knowledgeable men have acted differently, and it is of the greatest benefit to later generations for them to know as many examples as possible of those men who were most conscientious and wisest, and it is good for all to imitate them.

At every place he visited he preached himself or prompted someone else to do so when he had occasion to be away surveying his district. Various men were in his service, first of all the priest Þorkell Hallsson, a good and judicious preacher, who served for some years before he became a canon. In addition the priest Leggr served him for seven years, and later a northern priest named Bjǫrn, small in stature but wise and learned, and Bishop Brandr's foster-son. He later went abroad. Then the priest Brandr Dálksson served him, who had also served other bishops, Brandr and Guðmundr. The priest Ketill Hermundarson was also in his service prior to Bishop Páll's death, and he was responsible for the choir and the clerics in the church after the death of Bishop Páll. The aforementioned bishops had this man in their service, both of them, to show their steadiness and balanced disposition in this matter as in many others. Bishop Páll had various men in his service because it seemed to him better the more men were honoured and esteemed by him, and everyone's status was duly acknowledged while in his service, whatever came to pass later.

15. The Hostility between Bishop Guðmundr and the Northerners

At the time when Herdís died, the troubles among the northerners, Bishop Guðmundr and Kolbeinn Tumason, began. As is well known, all the men of the region suffered great distress, and Bishop Páll was most exposed to the trouble, such as had not occurred in the northern quarter before. He had come into such a difficult position in this affair that the archbishop had sent him sealed letters to the effect that he should support and strengthen to the best of his ability the case of Bishop Guðmundr, but many close friends of Bishop Páll supported Kolbeinn's case, his kinsmen and relations, to whom he [Páll] wished to show affection in every respect rather than causing them grief. It was not easy to reconcile these matters since Bishop Guðmundr thought he was not supported unless Bishop Páll stood up for him uncompromisingly because he honoured neither people nor the law and interdicted or excommunicated anyone who acted against his will. But Bishop Páll was in many ways an even-tempered man though not everything was done according to his lights, and he took care to profit many men by imposing light penalties, and then others were ashamed always to commit evil. Bishop Guðmundr was not so flexible with the people in Bishop Páll's district that he hesitated to interdict or excommunicate them the moment they made decisions not to his liking, though according to the law. But Bishop Páll did not let these words undermine people but assigned some little penance as a caution to them, those who were caught up in interdiction, because he wished his people to have some alternative rather than being in fear about whether they would be harmed or not.

But when the troubles had escalated to the point that they met in the battle in which Kolbeinn fell along with many other able men, both clerics and laymen, with some losing their limbs if they survived. And after that the bishop and his men attacked those who survived and were closest to Kolbeinn and drove them off and seized all their goods and declared them excommunicated. When Bishop Páll became aware and learned of these evils, he asked his friends not to launch a rapid attack on them. The reason for this was that he wanted to preclude that the nights of bloodshed should turn out to be, as the saying goes, the most impetuous, and he thought that matters would proceed more quietly and with greater prudence if some time were allowed to pass. On the other hand, he expected that Bishop Guðmundr would see the great calamity that had occurred and would offer good terms for honourable reconciliation with those who survived.

But when that was slow in coming and, on the contrary, it was learned that they were attacking men and committing robbery and inflicting wounds and were otherwise engaged in all sorts of misconduct, Bishop Páll sent his chaplain Bjǫrn to meet with Bishop Guðmundr and ask that he settle and defuse their troubles with compensation. He offered whatever support Guðmundr needed, provided he not forfeit his good will, and he offered material aid such as he had available, both in monetary and other contributions. It was easy to see in both initiatives—Bishop Páll's urging of the chieftains not to go north in the autumn when people's resentment was at its height and least moderated by sorrow over the heavy loss of men, and, in addition, the appeal to Bishop Guðmundr to grant those who survived, [Páll's] good and high-status kinsmen, an easier compensation for their dire losses than was now available—that he wished to save Bishop Guðmundr and his followers from danger while it was still possible. But Bishop Guðmundr did not agree to that and judged him to be partial to the chieftains in such an appeal. But it soon emerged what sort of wisdom attached to their projections, because that same year the chieftains went to Hólar and deposed Bishop Guðmundr from his seat and chased away much of the rabble living there, outlaws, robbers, and bandits. They killed some of them, and the nest of evildoers was uprooted, and from that time on there was good provision for good people. Bishop Páll invited Bishop Guðmundr with kindness and good will. He did not accept and avoided meeting him because he did not want to follow his good advice.

16. Concerning Gifts and the Manufacture of Precious Items

At that time Bishop Páll's son Loptr went abroad and paid visits to distinguished men in other countries, Bishop Bjarni in Orkney, then King Ingi in Norway, and his brother King Hákon.[1] From him he received honourable and precious gifts. And as the bishop sat in distress over [missing] his son and other tidings that had come to pass, God cheered him one summer with Loptr's return with

---

[1] Ingi was a candidate for king put forward by the Baglar party after 1197. He died in 1202. King Hákon is the aforementioned Hákon Sverrisson.

high honours and valuable gifts such as he had received, and he could report that his father's repute had stood him in good stead wherever he went.

During that summer the precious objects that Archbishop Þórir of Norway had sent to Bishop Páll arrived, a gilt crown such as never before had come to Iceland, a precious gold ring, and splendid gloves. The next summer when Bishop Páll had occupied his seat in Skálaholt for sixteen years, Nikulás, Bishop of Oslo, sent Bishop Páll a great golden ring weighing two ounces and set with a precious stone. And he sent him such a supply of balsam that there was little prospect that it would ever run low, and nothing else of such usefulness was so hard to come by. It had cost no less than several marks of refined silver.

It should also be mentioned that Bishop Páll sent his friends abroad many gifts, both falcons and other treasures. He sent Archbishop Þórir a bishop's staff of ivory fashioned so skilfully that no one had previously seen one made so well in Iceland. Margrét the Cunning had contrived it, and she was the most skilled carver in Iceland. She and her husband were at Skálaholt when Bishop Páll died and her husband, the priest Þórir, was charged with all the finances, while she carried out all of the bishop's orders. Bishop Páll had commissioned an altarpiece before he departed and allocated a great deal of gold and silver for the project, and Margrét carved ivory extremely well. There was every expectation that it [the altarpiece] would be the greatest treasure with his [Páll's] planning, and that Þorsteinn the cabinet maker and Margrét would perform well with their skills. Great dejection followed his death, and such matters came to a standstill in deference to a number of other concerns. Þorsteinn was commissioned to make the altar.

That same summer, the bishop's last, a cargo of timber for the vault [of the church] came from Norway, which Bishop Páll had caused to be felled. Then he handed over all the purchases for the church such as were needed to Þórir.

17. The Death of Bishop Páll

Now we have related those matters that turned out well that summer. But then I will report those matters that were very much to the contrary. There was a great earthquake the day after the observance for the people of Selja (July 8, 1211), and many people lost their lives. Many farm buildings collapsed, and that caused great damage. There was also a lack of dry weather entailing severe losses. In addition the death of Klœngr Þorvaldsson was reported, a man promising to be a great chieftain if he stayed alive.

That summer Bishop Páll suffered illness and great distress as he was circulating in the West Fjords, and he barely made it as far as Hítardalr. He was confined to bed for nearly four weeks. Then he returned home much depleted and got back to Skálaholt three days before Saint Simon's Day (October 25, 2011) and took to bed. He sang Mass on All Saints' Day (November 1), his last Mass to the glory of almighty God and all the saints, to implore help and mercy for himself and all Christians, both living and deceased. On Saint Martin's Day (November 11) his illness became acute with great pain, accompanied by both sleeplessness and loss of appetite, and he seemed to be at death's door. Present were his sons and brothers and many other of his dear friends.

Then Bishop Páll sent for Þorvaldr and Magnús, the sons of Gizurr, and they came to Skálaholt. He arranged everything for them according to his wishes. He was given the last rites eight days after Saint Martin's Day. Before he was given holy unction, he spoke at length after the example of Bishop Þorlákr the Saint. He confessed openly in the presence of all the clerics who were there, confessing all those wrongs of which he thought himself guilty during his episcopacy, and he asked them all to forgive him for his misdeeds against them. And he gently forgave all those who had wronged him and commended himself to God's mercy. After that he was anointed. There was some alleviation of his illness until he removed his clothing for the last rites and two days longer. Then the distress beset him anew and he lived no longer than two days after that. He took communion on his deathbed and then passed into the hands of God.

18. The Portents of Bishop Páll's Death

A week before Bishop Páll's death the moon turned blood-red and did not shine at midnight in clear weather, and that inspired great fear in many people.

Bishop Páll was consecrated bishop in the days of Pope Celestine by Archbishop Absalon, and in the days of King Sverrir. He was forty years of age. For sixteen years he guided God's Christian faith with great moderation and died on a Wednesday one day before Saint Andrew's feast day (November 30), and at that time there had passed 1204 [*recte* 1211] years since the birth of Christ.

The priest Ari the Wise, who has left a record of many learned matters, writes how greatly our country declined after the death of Bishop Gizurr (1082–1118), whom people accounted the wisest man in Iceland. But here may be seen what great foreboding anticipated the death of the glorious leader Bishop Páll: all the earth shook and trembled with fear; heaven and the clouds wept so that much of the earth's fruitfulness was spoiled; the heavenly bodies displayed signals of death when the last moments of Bishop Páll drew near, and the sea burned offshore. In the areas of his episcopate almost all the natural elements showed some sign of grief because of his death.

The last night of Bishop Páll's life Þorvaldr Gizurarson, a very wise chieftain, dreamed that Jón Loptsson consigned the flock that his son had guarded to the apostle Peter. And Jesus Christ consigned his flock to his Father before he was crucified, and God's mercy consigned this his flock to the apostle Peter before our father and guardian was called from us.

19. Bishop Páll's Posthumous Fame

Now one may see both the furthest reaches of this great bishop's episcopacy, and we believe that there are no people with a view of the end who are not more eager to see the beginning. And we, his admirers who survived, wish to assure ourselves that he has left behind almost all those virtues that people may have in memory of a good and distinguished man: worthy children with the prospect of making good the loss occasioned by the death of Bishop Páll; sufficient wealth and much church ornamentation, mostly complete and some undertaken with good prospects; good counsel in teaching conveyed constantly in words and the fair example of his life; generous support and enviable provision intended for all his close relations. He will have borne in mind that

God will comfort those for whom he could not provide in particular material consolation. This story of mine was bolstered by the wise man Ámundi Árnason, Bishop Páll's artisan, and he composed these stanzas:

> Wise lawman of the sun's Lord,
> Well did he lead the people
> For all of sixteen years
> Owning the bishop's see.
> Banisher of men's blots,
> Brisk in speech, is called away.
> In perfected peace may
> Páll soon join heaven's Ruler.
>
> The doer of God's deeds
> Deftly could govern law.
> Stout friend of laws strove
> Strong years for better things.
> We believe that his barter
> Pleased blessed God and men.
> He promoted men's profit
> Prompted by a good heart.
>
> All hold in high regard
> The open-handed man,
> Who prized peace for men
> With all-powerful God.
> We beg that our bishop,
> Who abates the lot of men,
> Soon may sparkle among
> The Alþingi of holy men.

20. The Death of Notable Men in the Days of Bishop Páll

During the sixteen years when Christianity was adorned under the blessing of Bishop Páll's episcopacy many important events transpired in the world. Among those who died were Pope Celestine, Archbishop Absalon, King Sverrir, the Norwegian kings Hákon and Guthormr, the Swedish kings Knútr and Sǫrkvir, the English king Richard, Bishop Njáll, Bishop Brandr, Bishop Jón, Jarl Haraldr in Orkney, Jarl Philippus, Abbot Einarr Másson, Abbot Guðmundr Bjálfason, Abbot Hafliði Þorvaldsson, and Abbot Þorkell Skúmsson. Many other distinguished men died during Bishop Páll's lifetime, both clerics and laymen: Jón Loptsson, Gizurr Hallsson, Sigmundr Ormsson, Þorleifr Þorláksson, Þorvaldr Þorgilsson, Kálfr Snorrason, Ari Bjarnarson, Ǫnundr Þorkelsson, Hermundr Koðránsson, Þórðr Snorrason, Guðmundr Ámundason, and the priest Bersi Halldórsson. There were many other events during his episcopacy: the loss of ships and eruptions on Hekla, hostile encounters, robberies and burnings, and many untoward deaths.

Now I have recapitulated with some haste the life of Bishop Páll, and inability is more to blame than ill will if this account is less outstanding than the subject on its own merits. May almighty God always grant him joy in eternal glory. Amen.

AN ACCOUNT OF THE PEOPLE AT ODDI

1. Bishop Þorlákr's Character

Blessed Bishop Þorlákr often conversed with wise and moral men, becoming acquainted with their honest customs and confirming them with his sound counsels so that they might persist in their goodness. He also held watch over the ways of those men who could not govern themselves in order to detach them from their wrongful desires, and he urged them to improve their ways, for our Lord declares: 'I do not wish the death of a sinful man but rather that he should mend his ways and live' (Ezekiel 33.11). And blessed Bishop Þorlákr showed all those who wished to repent of their failings and pay heed to his salutary counsel that he rejoiced in them and reproached them mildly with light penances. But as for those who did not wish to embrace God on the strength of his kind reminders or abandon their evil ways on the strength of his harsh rebukes, some of these he placed under interdiction and some he excommunicated according to the words of Christ to his disciples: You should reproach your brothers lovingly, 'but if they will not heed reproaches, then abhor them like heretics and heathens' (Matthew 18.17). He patiently endured the evil-doings of men but grieved greatly at their evil ways. He never condoned the immorality of wicked men, for he was eager to hear the words of God: 'Blessed are the patient at heart, for they will be called the children of God' (Matthew 5.9). But he was distressed by the disobedience of men and deeply regretted their spiritual wounds, so that no one experienced distress or grief without its affecting him as well because of his love of others.

Bishop Þorlákr made use of the governing power granted him by God in his consecration to loose and bind on God's behalf so that it seemed to wise people that he imposed penance with moderation, neither too harshly nor too gently, though he waited for many long and patiently if one looks closely. He often adverted to the words of King David in the psalter that the Lord loves mercy and justice and grants glory and kindness.

2. Þorlákr's Accession

Now since something has been said of the propitious conduct of this blessed bishop and no less of his episcopal authority and holy moderation, it is appropriate to listen to the words and events that attest how fitting it was that Þorlákr had a shepherd's name and was eternally reckoned among those bishops who adhered to the laws of almighty God in the highest degree and did not spare themselves from the sword of persecution even though God, who is all-powerful, allots for their protection both roses and lilies for their praise and glory. What we include is very little and limited because of our ignorance compared with the matter provided in his days of authority and supervision during fifteen years. And for that reason I will begin the story when he first came to Iceland as a new bishop.

3. Þorlákr's Progress in the East Fjords

When the holy Bishop Þorlákr had been in his see for a year, he began his oversight the second summer in the East Fjords. When he got south as far as Lómagnúpssandr, he was given hospitality at Svínafell. That was the residence of Sigurðr Ormsson, a great man in secular terms, wealthy and from a prominent family. The lord bishop was made welcome there as was appropriate. Because the owner wished to have his church consecrated, the bishop asked him to a meeting the following morning and conveyed the message of the Lord Archbishop Eysteinn to the effect that he had bidden him gather all churches and church resources in his episcopate under his authority.

Sigurðr was far from agreeing and said he would not relinquish what he had previously held freely by the custom of the land and ancient tradition.

The bishop said that the disposition of the apostles themselves gave him the authority over all God's possessions without any dispute: 'The holy Church fathers and popes, the successors of the apostles, have commanded and ordained the same thing in the laws of the Church throughout Christendom. Now the pope has ordered Archbishop Eysteinn to convey the same message in Norway, and that has been done. It is not right or tolerable that this poor land should not be subject to the same laws as in Norway.'

Sigurðr answered that 'Norwegians and foreigners cannot deprive us of our rights.'

Then the bishop replied: 'The disposition that foolish men have made to arrogate to themselves things they have already given to God is without force in law and should not be maintained. Inasmuch as this case is legally pleaded by bishops, these men are not numbered among those who can expect the help of God since they persist in this obstinacy. Anyone who stubbornly holds possession of tithes or the property of the clergy is excommunicable by legal admonition if they will not come to terms and refrain from their wrongdoing.'

The day advanced to the point that the property-owner saw that nothing would come of the church consecration unless he gave way. Now he made the wise choice and assigned the title of the church and the church itself to the authority of the bishop. Then the bishop consecrated the church and celebrated Mass. After the Mass he gave Sigurðr the church estate in fief for the time being and he assented to his maintaining it. From there the bishop went to Rauðalœkr. Ormr the Old lived there. He made the same claim as at Svínafell. The result was much the same, and Ormr put the management of the church in the hands of the bishop, who reassigned it to him, and they parted as friends.

Bishop Þorlákr went from there to the East Fjords on the same business, and most of the landowners had the same response, those who had church estates. Though many were slow to surrender their inheritances, it all came down to the same thing, and Bishop Þorlákr took over the management of all the churches east of Hjǫrleifshǫfði except at Þváttá and Hallormsstaðir, and that has remained in force ever since.

4. Concerning Jón Loptsson

At that time Jón Loptsson was in charge of Oddi and he was the greatest leader in Iceland. He was the owner of a chieftainship. He was very knowledgeable in clerical matters that he had learned from his elders. He was a deacon in orders and a powerful singer in the holy church. He was also much concerned that the churches under his authority should be well provided for in every way. He was also well versed in all the accomplishments practised by men at that time. He was such a great and commanding figure that scarcely anyone outdid him, for he wished to yield to no one or step back from what he had initiated.

AN ACCOUNT OF THE PEOPLE AT ODDI

He had a wife named Halldóra, the daughter of Brandr. Their son was named Sæmundr.

Jón was very enamoured of women and he had a number of other sons with various women, Þorsteinn and Halldórr, Sigurðr and Einarr. Páll, who later became a bishop, and Ormr, who later lived at Breiðabólstaðr, were his sons by Ragnheiðr Þórhallsdóttir, the sister of Bishop Þorlákr. They had been in love with each other from childhood, although she had children by several men. At that time Páll and Ormr, the sons of Jón and Ragnheiðr, had come of age when Bishop Þorlákr came to Iceland with his bishop's title. Páll lived at Ytra-Skarð, and Ormr at Breiðabólstaðr. Jón retained Ragnheiðr for a long time at home at Oddi.

At that time Jón had moved to Hǫfðabrekkuland, which people thought was one of the best properties before Hǫfðá flooded it. A southwesterly storm had wrecked two churches there, but now Jón had built a new church, which was very splendidly constructed. The holy Bishop Þorlákr was given hospitality there the autumn he returned from the East Fjords, as has already been told. The intention was that he should consecrate the church. A sumptuous feast was prepared to receive him. On the stipulated day he came with his company. Jón was in attendance with many other important men. In the morning the bishop prepared to consecrate the church, and Jón and those who took counsel with him approached the bishop to discuss how the church management should be arranged. The lord bishop asked, in accordance with legal provisions, whether Jón had heard the archbishop's orders with respect to church ownership. Jón replied: 'I can hear the archbishop's orders, but I am determined to discount them. Nor do I think that he has sounder wishes or knows better than my elders, Sæmundr the Wise and his sons. I will not disallow the procedures of our bishops in this country who approved the national custom that laymen were in charge of the churches which their ancestors gave to God while asserting control for themselves and their descendants.'

The bishop answered such arguments and many others, as described before, by saying: 'You know very well, Jón, if you will accede to the truth, that the bishop is to have charge of the church properties and tithes according to the ordinances of the apostles and other holy fathers, and because laymen cannot assert authority over these matters, that authority can never be justified on the basis of ancient custom. I expect that church leaders before our time took refuge in the fact that they were not commanded by their superiors to bring churches and tithes under their authority, but those who stubbornly withhold tithes or God's property against the will and license of the bishops are subject to excommunication.'

Jón replied: 'You can call anyone you want excommunicated, but I will never relinquish my property to your authority, neither my church nor anything else I have under my control.'

There was another dispute between them originating in the flooding of Hǫfðá, because it had wrecked many dwellings in its path, including two with churches. Because of that there was less in the way of tithes and fewer locations for services. For this reason Jón did not want more than one priest and one deacon per church, but before there had been two priests and two deacons. The bishop objected to this on the same grounds. With respect to the previous dispute each insisted on his way, and the day began to fade. Those who claimed to be the friends of both sides asked the bishop to relent and the people in general inclined the same way because of old habits.

When Bishop Þorlákr saw that he would not prevail for the moment, these are the words that sprang from his lips: 'Even though it is intolerable that it is judged right and proper that you should arrogate to yourself the control of the church according to national custom and dispossess the bishops, it is much more intolerable that the bishops cannot deprive you of your whores, with whom you consort against all national custom. It may be that you will persist in the greater evil if you persist in the lesser evil even if you are in the wrong.'

People think that Bishop Þorlákr spoke these words because he realised that popular opinion was on Jón's side in the church matter. He yielded for the moment because he saw no profit in pursuing the matter but great harm in more than one way, and he thought that later, with the aid of the archbishop, the church might come into its rights. But from the place where he expected to get relief bad news was in store because a little later Archbishop Eysteinn was exiled as a result of church disputes. People in Iceland thought they could follow the lead of what people did in Norway.

On this day the bishop consecrated the church and celebrated Mass even though his wishes did not prevail. He took the conclusion of the matter amiss. Others then followed the example of Jón and no one wished to surrender the churches to the authority of Bishop Þorlákr, and that put an end to his claims during his time.

There were many events during the days of Bishop Þorlákr that are worth recounting even though few are touched on here, for he endured all manner of trials and tribulations on various occasions because of the wickedness and disobedience of his charges, as may be heard in the episodes that follow.

5. The Problems at Bœr

A man named Hǫgni was living at Bœr in Borgarfjǫrðr. He was the son of Þormóðr, a priest in orders and very wealthy, but not of a distinguished family. His wife was named Geirlaug, and she was the daughter of Arnórr. Eyjólfr from Stafaholt was married to their daughter; he was a very wealthy man. Another daughter of Hǫgni was named Snælaug, and she remained at home without being married. She gave birth to a child whose father was identified as a worker named Gunnarr and who was given the nickname 'shepherd's dog'. Hǫgni was not upset with her for that reason and he esteemed his daughter no less than before this happened.

It came to pass that Snælaug was visiting at Saurbœr on Hvalfjarðarstrand. There the priest Þórðr, the son of Bǫðvarr at Garðar on Akranes, took a liking to her, and his heart went out to the woman. Þórðr and Bǫðvarr went to Bœr and asked Hǫgni for the woman's hand. The arrangement was made, and Snælaug was married to Þórðr. They loved each other very much and had a son together.

A man named Hreinn, the son of the Hermundr who lived at Gilsbakki, had been fostered at Hǫgni's farm at the time when Snælaug gave birth to a natural child. He had gone abroad, and the news of his death came from Norway. When Hǫgni and Snælaug learned of it, Snælaug said that Hreinn had been the father of her daughter

Guðrún, but she had not dared to reveal it because of his father Hermundr's power. When this became generally known, Þórðr and Hreinn proved to be fourth cousins. When Bishop Þorlákr became aware of this, he forbade Þórðr and Snælaug to be together, but because they were very much in love, they paid little heed to what he said.

This displeased Þórðr and Hǫgni to the point that they were totally hostile to the bishop and opposed to his counsels and criticisms. They assembled men to demonstrate their opposition. Hǫgni had gone to Norway for a cargo of timber and built a church at Bœr. Here a priest's fee had been paid no greater than twelve ounces. Hǫgni lost his [clerical] position because of the betrayal of those men he had assembled, the forbidden marriage, and his being in league with his son-in-law and daughter against the bishop in the aforementioned case. Bishop Þorlákr often talked about his wish to consecrate the church at Bœr, but Hǫgni knew that the bishop claimed the authority and control over all church finances and therefore he refused to allow the church ever to be consecrated as long as he had a voice in the matter of episcopal authority. He said that the church would be the most splendid horse stable in Iceland if he did not have his way. But the bishop turned down this possibility and did not refrain from proper condemnation, showing that he was not a shifting weathervane but rather a firm adherent to truth. He did not fear the menacing words and threats of these priests.

The aforementioned Eyjólfr was utterly opposed to the bishop because of his kinsmen and because the bishop had excommunicated him in a sex-related case. There was also a dispute pending because the bishop thought that Eyjólfr had wrongly taken over Stafaholt even though the men of the district had settled him there without consulting the bishop since the priest Steini had not given the property as an inheritance but assigned it to two impecunious women in his family as a permanent residence.

Now because the bishop was unyielding, Þórðr and Snælaug came to more or less of a settlement with him and accepted absolution and penance. The distribution of property and separation were arranged in such a way that Þórðr was to be at Garðar with his resources and Snælaug at Bœr with her resources. The resolution was no more effective than that Þórðr and Snælaug lived together for a long time and had three sons, Þorleifr, Markús, and Bǫðvarr. They were sometimes at peace with the bishop and sometimes under his interdiction.

The matter of church management was unresolved, and one time when the bishop was doing a visitation of the district, Eyjólfr lay in wait for him at Grímsá and seized his reins, not allowing him to proceed. The bishop did not wish to speak with him because he was excommunicated.

Eyjólfr spoke up and said: 'My business is to ask you to give me self-judgment in the case of two of your clerics who are my kinsmen at Bœr. They have a case of fornication to plead with respect to the daughters of landowners who are related to them. I have taken charge of this case.'

The bishop said not a word. Eyjólfr became angry and said: 'You and your men will not depart unscathed unless you give me self-judgment.'

There was a man named Þorleifr, nicknamed beiskaldi, who lived at Hítardalr and was in the company of the bishop. He saw that things were coming to a bad pass and

AN ACCOUNT OF THE PEOPLE AT ODDI   77

therefore he rode up to Eyjólfr and said: 'Would you like me to assign you self-judgment so that you can let the bishop proceed in peace?'

Eyjólfr said: 'You and the bishop are not comparable. I have no dispute with you.'

Þorleifr spoke: 'Many people will find my commitment acceptable, and if you do not accept it, we will both suffer disgrace.'

Eyjólfr accepted these terms and immediately imposed a fine of five hundred measures of russet homespun against each of the clerics, and they parted on those terms. From that time on Eyjólfr enjoyed neither good fame nor good fortune. His resources dried up, and he and his wife did not live long. His son Ari was struck down by leprosy and his daughter Ólǫf was a half-wit. He surrendered the management of Bœr (to Snorri Sturluson) with the agreement of Snælaug, and he was committed to marry her off and provide financing, but the marriage did not come about and she had children with vagabonds.

6. The Confrontation with Hǫgni and a Settlement

At one time the holy bishop Þorlákr was visiting at Reykjaholt with the priest Magnús. Magnús rode with a band of men south along the Múli heights together with the lord bishop, and as they separated he said: 'Today I know you will need reinforcement and for that reason I took many men with me. I want to accompany you until I know that you are out of danger.'

The bishop said: 'What is the source of the danger?'

Magnús replied: 'I have heard that Hǫgni in Bœr is displeased that you have excommunicated his kinsmen, Þórðr and Eyjólfr, and are unwilling to consecrate his church unless you can assume charge of the management, and he thinks his national rights have been breached. For that reason I think that he intends that you should stay at Bœr tonight and not at Saurbœr as you intended.'

The bishop replied: 'I thank you for your companionship and loyalty, but you should ride home and fare safely. Our trip is in the hands of God, and the people at Bœr will do us no harm.'

Magnús replied: 'I will do as you wish, but I wanted to tell you what the danger was and make my company available.'

The bishop replied: 'Farewell, good friend. God will watch over us.'

The people from Reykjaholt rode home, and the bishop rode ahead to Grímsá. Below the sandbanks there, at the place called Steinsvað, Họgni and his kinsmen were waiting with many men. As soon as the bishop and his men came to the declivity, Họgni's men rode up to them and barred their way.

The bishop asked why they were doing this. The priest Họgni then rode up and said: 'It is now my intention that you should consecrate the church at Bœr and go home with me.'

The bishop replied: 'I intended to go to Saurbœr and not to Bœr.'

Họgni said: 'I am in charge here and there are no alternatives.'

Bishop Þorlákr did not want to wait until he was taken into captivity and chose rather to go with this hostile band, and he spent the night at Bœr. But his determination was not swayed by their intimidation and he departed in peace with the leave of his enemies since they saw that he was prepared to endure any hardship rather than to bend the law with any sort of hypocrisy or cowardice. His opponents came to terms with his hostility when they saw his steadfastness. The wisest men were then enlisted as intermediaries on the property of the Church and a priest's compensation. Then the lord bishop saw that it was more important that many men in high standing, who were previously opponents of the Church, should take the Church's part even though Hǫgni had his demands about what privileges the Church had abroad rather than at home, since abroad it had unrestricted income. Both parties, Eyjólfr and Hǫgni and Þórðr and Snælaug, now received absolution. Thus Eyjólfr escaped the sex-related charges in which he had been mired.

After that the bishop returned to Bœr and was the recipient of a fine feast. There was a big crowd and lavish entertainment. The bishop consecrated the church with the management arrangements that Hǫgni and the bishop agreed on. On the concluding day of the feast Hǫgni gave the bishop honourable gifts and they had a friendly parting. From there Bishop Þorlákr went to Stafaholt. Eyjólfr made the bishop a gift of the money that Þorleifr had committed on his behalf. The lord bishop returned that autumn and settled with these men to ease the difficulties, and each was fully committed to the other.

Many men stood in strong opposition to Bishop Þorlákr, though some more openly than others, for they found him to be harsh and pitiless toward the people he found fault with for immorality and the patent crimes of evil men, and when he brought to bear the power and severity of the holy Church against those people who would not tolerate correction in the form of his well-intentioned representations.

7. The Case of Sveinn Sturluson

There was a man named Sveinn, the son of Hvamms-Sturla, an unruly and dishonest man. He took to his bed a close kinswoman of his wife. He lived in northern Reykjarfjǫrðr on the coast of the West Fjord quarter. Blessed Bishop Þorlákr very much disliked this state of affairs and condemned it, first with words and representations and then with interdiction and excommunication, because Sveinn was all the more persistent in his wickedness the more the bishop reminded him to mend his ways.

One time when the holy Bishop Þorlákr was visiting this quarter, this same Sveinn assembled men to ambush the bishop. They set out from home along the path they thought the bishop would follow. But when they had come a short way from his farm, a fog descended on them so that they could not see the way. When they had proceeded for a long while, they lay down at the spot where they were because of the lack of visibility, but the bishop and his men rode in bright light. At the moment when many men came out to meet the bishop, and Sveinn had not enough force to confront them, the fog lifted and they saw that they had gone astray and that the bishop had bypassed them so that they had no chance to catch him. Each of the ambushers accused the other of having gone astray. And because of this contention they incurred a great misfortune and they came to blows; Sveinn killed a man named Ǫrn by a pool there in the fjord. Both Sveinn and his companions got a quick and proper punishment for wishing to use force against a man of God. But the bishop and his men proceeded freely on their way according to their wishes.

8. Jón Loptsson and his Son Þorsteinn

The lord bishop Þorlákr litigated many matters with Jón Loptsson at Oddi concerning both sins of the flesh and wrongful appropriations, and especially the fact that he consorted with his [Þorlákr's] sister Ragnheiðr in his home with unmitigated obstinacy while his wife was still living. Though Jón responded in some manner to other charges brought by the bishop, on no account would he enter into an agreement to part with Ragnheiðr. It finally got to the point that the bishop placed Jón under interdiction. Jón was greatly distressed at suffering the harshness of the bishop because of his status, and in addition that many people took exception to their quarrel, especially his son Þorsteinn who lived at Gunnarsholt. He incited his father against the bishop with unheard-of foolishness. But Jón intended now as before to make the bishop compliant with intimidation rather than taking up arms against him.

One time when Bishop Þorlákr was carrying out his duties and his path led across the farm at Oddi, Jón thought to lay hands on the bishop and intimidate him as he had many others. He placed men on both sides of the path that led past the farm from the east, and they thought that the bishop would proceed that way because he was riding from the south from Eyjar and up toward Rangárvellir. When they crossed the eastern stretch of Rangá, it seemed to them that thick fog came up from the sea so that one could hardly see anything. The fog persisted until the bishop and his men were out of sight. Those lying in wait thought that the bishop must have gone a different way. The bishop's followers clearly saw that there were men in wait on both sides of the path. But because they did not know the reason, they proceeded fearlessly since the others offered no threat.

When Jón realised that his plan had come to naught, he rode home, circling around the bishop with the same intention and accompanied by some men. But he complained to his friends about how he should handle the hardships he felt he was suffering from the bishop.

His son Þorsteinn was with him and said: 'I will resolve the problem, father, and put an end to this bishop who behaves so atrociously toward men.'

Jón replied: 'You can meet with the bishop if you like, but you are destined to have a quite different misfortune than to convince Þorlákr to do anything. No one will succeed other than myself, if I put my mind to it.'

Þorsteinn said he was not convinced and proceeded in the company of some men. They came to Vellir when the bishop was sitting at a meal. When they saw men coming out, they asked where the bishop was. They were told that he was at table. Þorsteinn began to rail at the bishop in the event that he came out. Those who had come out went in again. They were asked who had arrived. They said that Þorsteinn Jónsson was there and men with him fully armed, and that Þorsteinn was making threats to harm him, should he emerge. The bishop had already been told his words and his father's reply and Jón's whole plan.

The householders discouraged the bishop from going out, but, steadfast and unafraid of the threats of evil men, he replied: 'I will go to church as I am accustomed. This man will do me no harm.'

The householders then said: 'Lord, sit inside and intone your psalter, and do not expose yourself to the weapons of this devilish man, who will stop at nothing.'

The bishop said: 'I will proceed as I intended. If this man does anything to me, it may be that I will need no additional help.'

After this the bishop went outside, and when Þorsteinn saw him, he did not hesitate to raise his axe, but it is not up to us to judge why he could not strike a blow, since we believe that it is God's power that hindered him. At that moment the bishop looked at him and said not a word and went to church as he intended.

Þorsteinn went to meet with his father and reported the outcome of his trip. Jón said: 'That is about what I thought would happen.'

He [Þorsteinn] was asked why he did not strike a blow with the axe. He said that his arm was paralysed from the moment the bishop looked at him until he came into the church so that he could not wield his axe.

9. The Confrontation between Jón Loptsson and Bishop Þorlákr

Jón Loptsson did not give up the hostility he had conceived and he assembled men and intended to ambush the bishop on the day he rode from Fellsmúli to Leirubakki at a place called Vatshlíð. He placed men on both sides of the way to the bathing site. The bishop had ridden from Vellir to Fellsmúli. News of Jón's plan was communicated to the bishop and his men, and people asked him to ride a different way so that they should not meet up. But he himself was steadfast and his steadfastness carried over to others; he feared neither numbers nor arms and rode undismayed toward the ambushers in waiting. But almighty God once again drew fog over the route he and his men took, and they advanced safely with a good view of the men in ambush. But Jón and his men did not see the bishop or his men or the path before the bishop and his followers had fallen out of view. The bishop rode the way he had intended that day and spent the night in hospitable quarters.

In the morning Jón knew that the bishop would ride to Ytra-Skarð. He intended to ambush him again, not on the road but at the farm at Skarð. He disposed men from the bathing site above Klofi along the whole way home to the church portal. Jón was to stand in it, and the bishop would not find his way to the farm without riding along the pathway or the churchyard and without Jón's being present. In the morning the plan was put into action. But before the bishop rode from Leirubakki, he learned of the measures taken by Jón. When they got to the bathing site, the bishop's men saw two serried ranks of men, between whom they were supposed to ride; they came to a halt.

The bishop caught up quickly and told them not to be afraid, 'for this game is being played against me, not you.' He was the first to ride the gauntlet, and his chaplain, the priest Ormr, was next after him, and then one after the other until the bishop got to the church portal where Jón was posted. Þorlákr dismounted. There was no chance of going through the portal because it was crowded with men. Nor was there a chance of turning back because the crowd pressed in from all directions. No greetings were exchanged.

The bishop said: 'Well, Jón, are you going to bar me from church?'

Jón replied: 'That's up to you.'

The bishop said: 'It seems to me that you want to make the rules now, and I am curious to know why you are doing this.'

Jón answered: 'You have kept me from church for a long time and vowed to excommunicate me. For that reason I would wish that when we meet, I might have the upper hand.'

The bishop said: 'It is true that I have declared an interdiction against you for good reasons and in that way have delayed the issue of excommunication so that I might hope that you have the wits to better your ways. But if you fail to do that, I will not put off excommunicating you, the sooner the better.'

'I know,' said Jón, 'that your excommunication is correct and the cause sufficient. I will endure your decision by going to Þórsmǫrk or some place not much frequented by people who consort with me and will remain with that woman whom you resent as long as I like, and your excommunication will not resolve my difficulties, nor will the main force of any man until such time as God inspires me to put my problems behind me by my own good will. Make up your mind that I will bring it about that you will not impose your decree on anyone but me.'

At these words the bishop became silent for a time, but he finally spoke up: 'I am prepared to accept whatever is my lot in this matter. Do what you wish because I am determined not to forego the edict of excommunication because I fear your threats.'

Jón retorted: 'If this is your intention, I will not risk further meetings with you.'

Even though Jón spoke in this way, the bishop was not at all intimidated. But the priest Ormr, who stood by him, could see that Jón would not relent in his anger and that those who had previously incited hostility were quite prepared to carry out their threats. He pressed in front of the bishop and said: 'I entreat you, lord, in the name of our Lord Jesus Christ, not to bring down excommunication on Jón and your sister just now. You should rather wait for that moment, which Jón has led us to expect, when he will separate from her and accept your remedy. Consider, lord, whether you think this forbearance involves a great humbling of the Church or whether it is not a greater humbling to lose you both on the same day, for Jón is surely to be relied on to keep his word when he makes a good promise. Even though you are putting your life at risk on God's behalf, see to it that the smaller crime is not paid for with a greater crime in its wake; it is better to wait patiently for what is good than to exacerbate the difficulties.'

The bishop at first gave him a stern look. But because many others supported his message, the bishop said: 'Now as before, Jón, you are determined to be in charge, even though you are wrong. But if I could be sure that the delay would turn out well, I would risk it.'

All those who were present were cheered by his allowing a delay of the excommunication, and in this way the bishop escaped with his life.

After that Jón was asked when the mending of his ways would take place, such as he had put in prospect if the bishop delayed excommunication. Jón replied: 'It is up to the bishop to promise whether the waiting time will be uneventful, and I will have to determine the end of the matter.'

The conclusion of this meeting was that the bishop promised not to exacerbate hostilities with Jón for some time, and Jón allowed the bishop into the church and rode away. After that a few months passed before Jón relinquished Ragnheiðr, and they accepted absolution and penance from the bishop. A little later Ragnheiðr was married to a Norwegian named Arnþórr, and many people are descended from them. But the bishop stayed aloof from Jón and Ragnheiðr for his whole life so that they would not have any encounters or conversation except in the presence of witnesses and in public places. There were never anything but unfriendly relations between the bishop and Jón for as long as they both lived. Þorsteinn, Jón's son who wished to kill Bishop Þorlákr, as has been related, turned out to be a most luckless fellow so that his father and brothers suffered repeated provocations because of him.

10. The Last Days of Jón Loptsson

Some time after these events Jón had a church and cloister built north of the brook [that runs] north of Keldur and intended to retire there himself, but none took up residence there.

When Bishop Þorlákr heard news of this, he pretended not to know and asked whether Jón intended to build a cloister at Keldur. He was told that that was the case. Then he asked further: 'To what holy man does he intend to dedicate the cloister?'

Those who were with him said that he intended to dedicate the cloister to John the Baptist.

The bishop said: 'It is a great miracle if he will accept what has been accumulated there considering how it was amassed.'

These words were not without significance because when Jón came to Keldur, he quickly fell ill, and when it began to slow him down, he had himself brought to the door. When he looked at the church, he said: 'There you are, my church. You grieve for me, and I grieve for you.'

He seemed to see that the building of the church was uncertain if he was called away. After his death his son

Sæmundr had the dilapidation of the church and buildings repaired. When he was gone, his sons divided the church and dismantled buildings as their paternal inheritance, and the words of the holy bishop, Þorlákr, were revealed as they were recorded above.

THE PRIESTHOOD OF BISHOP GUÐMUNDR GÓÐI

1 The Ancestry of Guðmundr góði

Þorgeirr Hallason lived below Hvassafell in Eyjafjǫrðr. He was married to Hallbera Einarsdóttir from Reykjanes. Einarr was the son of Ari, who was the son of Þorgils, the son of Ari, the son of Már. Þorgeirr and Hallbera had ten children who survived infancy, five sons and five daughters.

One of their sons was Einarr. He had no children. He lost his life in the wilderness of Greenland, and there are two stories about it. One of them is from Styrkárr Sigmundarson from Greenland (he was a great and truthful storyteller), to the effect that their ship had ended up in the wilderness. The crew had separated and come to blows because one group had run short of rations before the other. Einarr had got away with two other men and went in search of habitation. He went up onto the glaciers, and they perished a day's distance from habitation. They were found a year later. Einarr's corpse was whole and unscathed, and he is buried at Herjólfsnes.[1]

Another of Þorgeirr's sons was named Þorvarðr. He went abroad at the age of eighteen. As soon as he planted his feet in Bergen, he struck down a follower of King Ingi named Jón so that he never recovered and died the following winter. The motivation was that this man had left him in the lurch in Eyjafjǫrðr. But Þorvarðr immediately took passage on another ship and they arrived in Bergen three days later than Jón. Þorvarðr took refuge with Ketill Kálfsson and

---

[1] Herjólfsnes is a settlement in Greenland a little to the northwest of the southern tip.

had in hand both the axe and the handle that had broken when he struck Jón. The matter concluded with Þorvarðr's becoming King Ingi's follower and gaining his affection. That completes the story of Þorvarðr's actions because there is more material than I wish to include in this saga.

He married when he brought his travels to an end and took to wife Herdís Sighvatsdóttir. He had five daughters who survived infancy. One was Guðný, who was married to Þorgeirr, the son of Bishop Brandr, and later she was married to Eiríkr Hákonarson from Orkney, the grandson of Sigurðr slembir;[1] another was Gyðríðr who was married to Kolbeinn Tumason; a third was Guðrún who was married to Klœngr Kleppjárnsson; a fourth was Hallbera who was married to Þórðr Ǫnundarson; and the fifth was Ingibjǫrg who was married to Brandr [Knakansson].[2]

Before Þorvarðr was married he had a daughter with Yngvildr, the daughter of Þorgils Oddason. She was married to Hjálmr Ásbjarnarson. He had another daughter with Herdís Klœngsdóttir, and her name was Helga. She was married to Teitr Oddsson in the East Fjords. Þorvarðr had a son named Ǫgmundr with a woman whose name was Helga. Ǫgmundr Þorvarðsson was married to Sigríðr Eldjárnsdóttir at Espihóll. In his old age Þorvarðr had a daughter named Berghildr with Birna Brandsdóttir. She was married to Eldjárn from the Fljótsdalr district.

Þorgeirr's third son was Þórðr, who was a monk at Þverá and died there. He had no children. The fourth

---

[1] Sigurðr slembir was a pretender to the throne of Norway and was killed in 1139. According to *Morkinskinna* (2011), II, 173–174; *Morkinskinna* (trans.) (2000), 369 he spent a winter in Iceland.

[2] A note in *Sturlunga saga* (1946), 546, identifies this Brandr as Brandr Knakansson, who is mentioned in *Guðmundar saga dýra,* chapter 10 (ibid., 178), though without his patronymic.

son was named Ingimundr. He was married to Sigríðr Tumadóttir and had no children. He was a priest and a very distinguished man. Ari was the fifth son of Þorgeirr. He was a big, strong man.

Heðinn Eilífsson, who lived at Hólar in Eyjafjǫrðr, was married to Þóra Þorgeirsdóttir. Later she was married to Eyjólfr Einarsson. Another of Þorgeirr's daughters was Ingibjǫrg. She was first married to Helgi Eiríksson from Langahlíð and later on to Hvamm-Sturla. Þorgeirr's third daughter was named Þórný. She was married to Grímr Snorrason at Hof in Skagafjǫrðr on Hǫfðastrǫnd. A fourth daughter of Þorgeirr's was named Gríma. She was married to Brandr Tjǫrvason at Víðivellir. A fifth daughter of Þorgeirr was named Oddný. She was married to Darr-Þórir Þorvarðsson.

A man named Gunnarr was called Sledge-Gunnarr. He was the son of Helgi, who was the son of Þórðr, who was the son of Þórir, who was the son of Arngeirr, who was the son of Bǫðvarr. Gunnarr was married to Rannveig, the daughter of Úlfheðinn, who was the son of Kolli, the son of Þormóðr, the son of Kolli, the son of Þorlákr, the brother of Steinþórr from Eyrr, from whom the Eyrbyggjar are descended. Þormóðr Kollason was married to Þórný Aradóttir from Reykjanes.

Gunnarr and Rannveig had a daughter named Úlfheiðr. She was married against her will. Sometime later Ari Þorgeirsson took a liking to her and had four children with her. They had a son named Klemet who died young. They had another son named Guðmundr. He was born at the residence in Hǫrgardalr called at Grjótá. At that time Steinunn, the daughter of Þorsteinn and Sigríðr Úlfheðinsdóttir lived there. She was a cousin of Úlfheiðr and they were on affectionate terms. It was three days before Michaelmas when a boy was born (September 26, 1161). The wise and learned man Guðmundr kárhǫfði was present. When the newborn child's voice sounded, he said that he had not heard such a child's voice and declared that he knew for a fact that this child would outshine all other men if he lived long enough. He said that he felt great awe at the sound.

They had a daughter named Guðrún and a son Gunnarr, who died young. When Ari and Úlfheiðr were joined, she transferred the value of fifteen hundreds in regular currency to his management and supervision. But she held onto a gold ring and many other valuables. But because Ari was a lavish spender, this money was quickly used up.

2. The Story of Ari Þorgeirsson

Now the story picks up at the point where Þorvarðr Þorgeirsson came from Norway after the fall of King Ingi and declared that he did not wish to serve any earthly king after King Ingi because he thought that none would be his equal. He asked his brother Ari, in the event that he went to Norway, not to join the group that had brought King Ingi down and predicted that a faction would rise up in the east in Vík to seek revenge, and he asked him to join that faction and take his own place in it.

Now Ari went abroad and Úlfheiðr stayed behind with their son Guðmundr. Ari made his way to Jarl Erlingr and found him to the east in Vík in the spring. Hákon herðibreiðr and Jarl Erlingr soon met in battle in Túnsberg, and Hákon suffered a defeat and fled.[1] A little

---

[1] Hákon herðibreiðr was king of Norway at a very young age (1157–1162) but never had a secure position.

later they fought at Hrafnabjǫrg and Hákon was again put to flight. They fought a third battle that summer off Sekkr in Raumsdalr. King Hákon fell there, and many outstanding men with him.

Jarl Erlingr accorded Ari great honour for his allegiance. In the winter the jarl travelled to Upplǫnd with King Magnús and Ari and many followers. They fought a battle at Reyrr a short distance from Hamarkaupangr, and they fought against Jarl Sigurðr.[1] He fell there, and many troops with him.

When news reached Iceland of what honour Ari earned from the king and jarl, Þorvarðr recited a stanza:

> My brother fierce in battle
> Stood bravely under full shields
> Eagerly with Erlingr
> In early summertime.
> A young recruit kept both
> Our common places, where
> Dark-coloured cuirasses
> Were cut away and split.

In the spring Ari was keen to return to Iceland, and the jarl gave him a fully outfitted vessel. He had a good sea voyage and arrived at Gásir in Eyjafjǫrðr. The ship was shared equally with Ámundi Koðránsson.

That summer was known as the stone-barrage summer. A battle was fought at the Alþingi, and many men were injured. The priest Halldórr Snorrason fell there and Þorvarðr Þorgeirsson was wounded. When these things came about, it seemed to the chieftains urgent to extend the Alþingi meeting so that these matters could be litigated

---

[1] This is Sigurðr Hávarðsson af Reyri, who figures in the stories of Hákon herðibreiðr and Magnús Erlingsson in *Heimskringla,* see *Heimskringla* (1951), III, 459, *Heimskringla* (trans.), III, 285.

since men had been injured with stonecasts and weapons. It seemed most extraordinary with respect to stone throwing, according to truthful men who were there, since after the battle men could scarcely lift the stones that were launched in the battle.

When the matter of extending the meeting had been much discussed, Þorgeirr Hallason took it on himself to respond and spoke as follows: 'It is a certainty that I am not in agreement with the idea of causing everybody so much trouble and inconvenience by extending the Alþingi, and I fear lest in the process the problems and hostilities grow rather than diminish. The wisest of men have taught us to quell problems, not stir them up. Now my son has become the victim of injuries, and I think him a worthy man, but I will not make him the cause, or myself either, of difficulties for the people. Rather, I will wait and take counsel and return home for the time being.' When he had made this announcement, all the chieftains concurred, and the Alþingi was disbanded.

In the autumn Ari took up residence with his father at Hvassafell, and Úlfheiðr went with him. They stayed there for two years. Their son Guðmundr had come as well. When Ari had been there for two years, he went abroad with his brother Ingimundr. When they reached land, Ari took up residence with Jarl Erlingr's retinue and stayed with him over winter (1165). During that winter the faction of Óláfr Guðbrandsson came into being; he was the grandson (half-brother?) of Haraldr gilli.[1] Ari fitted out his ship in the spring for Iceland, and they were

---

[1] Óláfr Guðbrandsson raised an insurrection against Erlingr skakki but succumbed to an illness in 1169. His story is told briefly in *Heimskringla* (1951), III, 407–410; *Heimskringla* (tr.), III, 255–256.

THE PRIESTHOOD OF GUÐMUNDR GÓÐI 97

ready to sail. Those who envied Ari most slandered him with the charge that he adhered to his allegiance with Jarl Erlingr by leaving him when he most needed men and when war was most imminent. When Ari learned of this talk, he had his belongings removed from the ship and rejoined the court retinue with the king and jarl. But the priest Ingimundr and the other Icelanders set out for Iceland and had a safe voyage. That summer Ari was in the jarl's retinue, and in the autumn to the east in Vík.

The night after All Saints' Day (November 2, 1166) the jarl was located at the place called Ryðjǫkull with his men. During the night he got up according to habit for matins and went to church with the men who were closest to him. After matins the jarl continued to sit and sing psalms. Then they heard trumpets blaring and thought that they could detect that there was an armed attack in the offing. The jarl finished his psalm and then went out; they realised that an armed force was approaching the residence so that it was crowded with men. The jarl wanted to return to his quarters, where his men and weapons were located. Then Bjǫrn bukkr spoke up, saying that the jarl should obviously flee, that they could not protect him even though they wanted to. Ari replied: 'Here we are, and let us defend the jarl all the more readily because there are no weapons.'

Then they retreated with the enemy on their heels. Bjǫrn bukkr and Ívarr gilli, both men of high standing, Bjǫrn the Marshall, and Ari all supported the jarl. When they came to a certain fence, Bjǫrn bukkr and Ívarr gilli leapt over it, but the jarl could not clear it because he was heavy. Bjǫrn and Ívarr helped him over it. But Ari put himself between the jarl and the enemy and shielded the jarl. He faced the onslaught and thus saved the jarl's life with his presence because he was not wounded up to that time. Then he was struck by a thrust to the throat and was pinned to the fence. Ari lost his life there, but the jarl escaped though he was wounded in the thigh before he got over the fence. In this attack ten men fell in addition to Ari.

These are the jarl's men who fell according to the report of Þorkell hagi: Ari Þorgeirsson, Einarr opinsjóðr, Bjǫrn sterki, Jón fjósi, Ívarr dœlski, Gunnarr tjǫrskinn, and Þóroddr Jórsalamaðr.

When the jarl got over the fence and out of harm's way, he asked where the Icelander Ari was. They said he was left behind dead at the fence. The jarl replied: 'It is a certainty that there went the man who served us best, and we have no one of such bravery left. He was the only one among you prepared to give his life voluntarily for mine. Now I will not be able to compensate his kinsmen for the loss they have suffered on my behalf.' Now the jarl gets to his troops and gathers his forces and arranges for the burial of the men who had fallen. This news reached Iceland the following summer. Then his brother Þorvarðr composed a dirge about Ari, thinking that the greatest comfort for Ari's death would be to commemorate his valour in verses that would be widely circulated.

3. Bishop Bjǫrn and Bishop Brandr

Now I will pick up the story at the point where Ari's son Guðmundr was born at Grjótá. The fall of King Ingi and the burning of Sturla's residence at Hvammr both happened at the same season. At that time Bjǫrn was the bishop at Hólar and Klœngr was the bishop at Skálaholt. Archbishop

Eysteinn had been consecrated the previous year, and 1161 years had passed since the birth of our Lord.

The next summer Bishop Bjǫrn went north to Þverá to consecrate his brother Bjǫrn as abbot. During that trip he confirmed Guðmundr Arason at Mǫðruvellir, and that took place in the spring after Easter.

That summer Bishop Bjǫrn intended to ride to the Alþingi, but he fell ill so that he could not make it to the Alþingi. He summoned his kinsmen and friends and made the arrangements he thought most needful because people realised, as was later revealed, that he was aware that he should prepare for his death. He gave a hundred hundreds of church property to Munkaþverá, and by doing that he showed both that he thought he had not been lavish with church funds and that he believed the best way to strengthen Christianity was to strengthen monastic life. He empowered his kinsman Brandr, who became his successor, to collect the money. It was done with foresight to empower the person who was himself designated to make payment. Then he went to Hólar and was bedridden all summer and died in the autumn the day before the commemoration of the eleven thousand virgins of Cologne.[1]

Then Þorgeirr Hallason offered to foster Guðmundr Arason. That was in the second year of his life. At that time King Hákon herðibreiðr fell off the island of Sekkr and Magnús became king.[2] That was the time of year

---

[1] A legend recounts that 11,000 virgins were martyred in Cologne in the fourth century. See the *New Catholic Encyclopedia* (2003), vol. 14, 345 s.v. Ursula, St.

[2] The story of the battle off Sekkr is told in *Heimskringla* (1951), III, 381–383 and *Heimskringla* (trans.), (2016), III, 238–240.

when Abbot Ásgrímr and Þorvaldr the Wealthy died. It was also the time when men fought at the law court south in Flói and when Hrói was consecrated bishop in the Faroe Islands (1163). The next season Ari Þorgeirsson came from Norway, and that summer there was a battle at the Alþingi, as previously related. In the summer Brandr Sæmundarson was elected bishop and went to Norway.

The next season after that Þorgeirr and his sons recruited many men for the Alþingi. Ari had many Norwegians in his company, almost thirty, and this was called the summer of shields. Father and son prosecuted the case against the people of Vatnsfjǫrðr for the wounding of Þorvarðr, and they pursued the case to the extent that the man who struck the blow was outlawed. The people from Vatnsfjǫrðr, Páll and Snorri, gave Þorvarðr self-judgment. Þorkell Flosason, who had been outlawed during the summer, surrendered his head to Þorvarðr on Holy Thursday in the evening and laid it on the table before him. He spared his head and bade him depart in peace wherever he wished, and he gave him a horse after Easter and told him that he should have the benefit of coming at that season of the year.

The following season (1165) Bishop Brandr came from Norway. There were great earthquakes on Grímsnes, and eighteen men perished. There was a tempest[1] on the commemoration day for Pope Gregory (1166). The season after that Ari Þorgeirsson fell and Christ's blood came to Trondheim.[2] That year Jón Sigmundarson the Elder died. Abbot Hreinn was consecrated.

---

[1] The word that I have translated 'tempest' is *Karlshríð* and is unexplained. See *Sturlunga saga* (1946), chapter 3, note 3 (p. 546).

[2] Christ's blood must indicate a relic of some kind.

4. Ingimundr Þorgeirsson Fosters Guðmundr Arason

In the seventh year news arrived from Norway about Ari's fall. And because Ari's property did not come into the hands of his son Guðmundr, his kinsmen thought the best thing for him was to study.[1] The priest Ingimundr took him under his care for instruction and the first installment of his compensation for his father and his inheritance was to be beaten to book learning. He was very resistant, and it seemed clear in his conduct that he would take after his family in intransigence because he wanted to have the last word with anyone he dealt with. For that reason his foster-father was a hard taskmaster.

That winter (1167) was known as the weird winter because many strange things occurred. Two suns were sighted at the same time. There was a sighting of elves and other strange creatures riding together in Skagafjǫrðr—and it was Ari Bjarnarson who saw them. It happened on Hegranes that a young sow ran out of her sty at night, broke down a door, and ran up to a bed in which a mother and child were sleeping. The sow seized the child and bit it to death, then ran out. The child was left dead and the sow ran back to her sty.

The next season after that Þorgeirr sold Hvassafell and moved to Munkaþverá; Þorvarðr and the priest Ingimundr then took over the household. At that time (1169) the church at Laufás burned. Guðmundr was then eight years old. Guðmundr and his foster-father Ingimundr travelled north to Háls to stay with Brandr, who was married to Gríma Þorgeirsdóttir, and they spent half a year with him. Then Þorvarðr moved the household to Ljósavatn. Guðmundr spent nine years there.

---

[1] Christianity brought with it the opportunity for unpropertied young men to study for the priesthood.

At that time Ingimundr resided with his kinsman Brandr at Háls. That year Þorvarðr killed Hǫskuldr Herason, and the killing of Kárr Koðránsson [and Bǫðvarr Grímsson] took place.¹ Karl [Jónsson] was consecrated as abbot of Þingeyrar. At that time Guðmundr was ten years old. His foster-father went to live at Vaglar, and Þorvarðr went to live at Háls.

When the brothers thus lived in the same neighbourhood, Guðmundr and Qgmundr were playmates together with a good many other young fellows. Their play always turned out the same way no matter how it began, to wit, that Guðmundr got the mitre and crozier and priestly garb, the church and altar, and he played the part of the bishop while Qgmundr got the axe and shield and other weapons and took the part of the warrior.² People thought this was very prophetic when what was destined for each was fulfilled.

At that time eighty men perished in a landslide, and it was called a portentous winter. In this period Archbishop Thomas [of Canterbury] fell in England, and the monk Þorgeirr Hallason died (1172). In the summer Einarr Helgason and the forest boys together with Vilmundr Snorrason, who was the son of Kálfr, fought at Saurbœr; eight of Vilmundr's men fell, and Einarr was wounded and carried off on a shield. Some of the men in his following were also wounded.³

The following spring the priest Ingimundr moved to the lower Mǫðruvellir and rented the land for ten

[1] This killing is reported in *Sturlu saga* in *Sturlunga saga* (1946), chapter 16 (p. 84); trans. Julia H. McGrew (1970), I, 81.

[2] Cf. *Óláfs saga helga,* ÍF 27, 107–108; *Heimskringla* (trans.), II, 68–69.

[3] They were called 'forest boys' because they had been outlawed. See *Sturlu saga* in *Sturlunga saga* (1946), chapter 16 as in note 1 above.

hundreds (1172). At that time Ingimundr married Sigríðr Tumadóttir. That autumn Sturla Þórðarson and Einarr Þorgilsson did battle on Sælingsdalsheiðr because Einarr had plundered Sturla's kinsman Ingjaldr.[1]

When Guðmundr was twelve years old, Ingimundr moved west to Skagafjǫrðr and took up residence with his kinsman Tumi at Áss together with his wife Sigríðr because their relationship was not easy. Guðmundr joined Þorvarðr at Háls. That spring Ketill from Grund died.

In the autumn Ingimundr moved away from Áss because he and Sigríðr did not manage together. Many outstanding men invited him, but he went to live with Hallr Hrafnsson at Grenjaðarstaðir. His kinsman Guðmundr moved there in the spring at Lent. That was known as the good winter. Saint Sunnifa had been translated from Selja during the previous summer. When her coffin was brought toward a fire, it arrested the blaze. Einarr Grímsson was killed and Helgi Skaptason's dwelling was burned at Saurbœr on Kjalarnes. Styrkárr Oddason became lawspeaker.

5. Ingimundr and Guðmundr at Grenjaðarstaðir

Now Ingimundr and Guðmundr stayed for four years at Grenjaðarstaðir. Guðmundr was twelve years old when he was ordained by Bishop Brandr as an acolyte. A year later Bishop Brandr made him a subdeacon and at the age of fourteen a deacon. The first year thereafter it happened that Ingimundr Jónsson, the brother of Abbot Karl Jónsson, was killed. That year Páll Þórðarson left Vatnsfjǫrðr with Sveinn Sturluson and together with

---

[1] The robbing of Ingjaldr's sheep and the battle on Sælingsdalsheiðr are told in *Sturlu saga*, chapters 20–21, in *Sturlunga saga* (1946), 89–94; trans. Julia H. McGrew (1970), I, 86–91.

a large number of men went to Helgafell and abducted Hallgerðr Rúnólfsdóttir and her daughter Valgerðr (1175). A year later Helgi Skaptason was killed at the Alþingi because he had burned the merchant ship belonging to the Norwegian Páll, who was called Burnt Páll. After that killing Þorvarðr led the prosecution and was given self-judgment against the Norwegians, and his reputation was much enhanced. That year Snorri Kálfsson at Mel died.

The next year Bishop Klœngr died. Then King Eysteinn [meyla] fell at Ré [Ramnes] and Nikulás Sigurðarson as well.[1] That year saw the quarrel of Arnórr Kolbeinsson and Sveinn Sturluson. Sveinn had ridden to visit the woman to whom Arnórr barred access. Arnórr rode after him with six men and fought against him on the later feast day of Saint Mary at the edge of Svínavatn (September 8). Sveinn was with another man, and his companion was seized and restrained, but Sveinn ran at Arnórr and struck at his arm so that he was unable to fight. The six others went after him and thought they had left him for dead. But Sveinn recovered from his wounds and lived on in a disabled state.

From this account we may see that Arnórr took after Kolbeinn in not restraining his passion and fury even on the feast day of Mary. The second year after that (1178) Bishop Þorlákr the Saint was consecrated. Sverrir was named king. Guðmundr was seventeen years old.

6. A Shipwreck

At that time Guðmundr and Ingimundr moved away from Grenjaðarstaðir, and Ingimundr went to Staðr in Kaldakinn

[1] On Eysteinn meyla see *Heimskringla* (1951), III, 414–416; *Heimskringla* (trans.) (2016), III, 259–260.

to live with Þórarinn. He lived there for two years. But Guðmundr moved down to Saurbœr in Eyjafjǫrðr to stay with Óláfr Þorsteinsson; he spent two years there while his foster-father was at Staðr.

The previous year Guðmundr kárhǫfði had had a vision. That year was the first in which Bishop Þorlákr occupied his see. Jarl Erlingr fell the following spring (1179). The feast days for Saint Ambrose, Saint Cecilia, and Saint Agnes were legally instituted and two days were dropped from the week of Pentecost. The following year Hallbera Einarsdóttir died. Then Guðný Þorvarðsdóttir was married to the bishop's son Þorgeirr, and the wedding feast was held at Háls. There were six hundred wedding guests. That year saw the battle between Sverrir and Magnús at Íluvellir (1180).[1]

In the spring when Guðmundr was nineteen years old, the priest Ingimundr prepared to go abroad, and his foster-son Guðmundr along with him. They arranged for passage at Gásir with Hallsteinn kúlubakr and set sail the day before Michaelmas (September 28). That was a Sunday, and the wind carried them north past Gnúpar to Melrakkaslétta. Then a contrary wind sprang up and they wallowed for a week westward toward Hornstrandir.

One evening when they were sitting at mealtime and a man named Ásmundr, a Norwegian, was spreading protective canvas, he looked out and exclaimed: 'Devils and damnation, down with the canvas. Up and at them, the breakers are on us. Stow the tables and pay no heed to the food.' Men jumped up and threw down the canvas.

Then the commander Hávarðr called out: 'Where is our ship's priest?'

---

[1] The battle at Íluvellir is described in *Sverris saga* (2007), 71–76.

'Not hard to find,' said Ingimundr, 'what is it you want from him?'

'We want to confess.'

He said: 'Confession is no better now than in the autumn when I urged you every Sunday in the name of God and you paid no attention. Now it is of no importance that God should hear your confession because the sea is on top of me as much as on you. Be of good courage and fearless.'

They answered: 'Now, priest, you will want to vow a pilgrimage to Rome and make other great vows, for now nothing else will suffice.'

'Not at all,' said the priest, 'I will make a vow if I am allowed to determine the content. But otherwise I will speak for all the Icelanders on board and no one will participate in any vows with you, for I no more want your concern for me than you wanted my concern for you last autumn.'

'How will you frame your vow, priest?'

'I will vow in the name of almighty God and the holy cross and Saint Mary and all the saints to give a tenth of all that is salvaged on land to the churches or the poor according to the disposition of the bishop.'

They reply: 'It is up to you, priest, for now we cannot do without your protection.'

They joined hands around the ship in support of this vow. By now they had got very close to the breakers and there was a great dispute about what to do. Everybody wanted to get his own way. Some of them wanted to raise the sails, and there was a rush to do it. Then the commander Hávarðr addressed Ingimundr the priest and asked him if he knew the highest name of God.

He answered: 'I know some names of God, and I believe what the apostle Paul said, to wit that there is no higher or holier name of God than Jesus. But I don't know what you refer to as "highest".'

He answered: 'People who do not know the name of God I would not call priests.'

Then he called to the steersman Hallsteinn and asked: 'Do you know the highest name?'

He replied: 'God knows that I think it has dropped out of my mind, and that is a bad thing, but Þórðr Crow will know.'

'Þórðr Crow, do you know the name?'

He answered: 'More is the shame, mate—it has escaped my memory. But I know somebody else who will know, and that will be Þorbjǫrn Hops.'

'Well then, Þorbjǫrn Hops, name the name if you know it.'

He answered: 'I wish I could, but I think I have never heard the name. But I will refer you to the man who, I think, will remember, Einarr nefja.'

The question was put to him, and he named the name.

When they had lifted the sail from the cargo to a level not quite the height of a man, there came a great wave at the cargo from the stern and bow and washed over the cargo. Every man clung to a rope. Ingimundr the priest took hold of the boat hook and wanted to pull down the sail, but his foster-son Guðmundr was busy with the lifeboat and stood between the boat and the sail trying to ease the sail up. At that moment another wave struck, of such size that the ship suddenly keeled over and knocked the pennant down along with the railing boards. It knocked everything loose in the cargo and overboard, except for the men. The ship was badly damaged and the lifeboat too. They pitched forward over the breaker and suffered the impact of a third wave, which was less weighty than the others. Then there was a rush to bail both fore and aft, and the sail was hoisted. Now they saw land and speculated on where they were. Some said that they had come to Málmey. Þórarinn rosti, an Icelander, said it had taken too much time for that.

Then Már Eyjólfsson said he could recognise that they had drifted to Hornstrandir and Skjalda-Bjarnarvík, and he said he had been there during the summer. They asked him to show the way to a harbour, and they wanted to sail north to Þaralátrsfjǫrðr because a secure harbour was located there.

Then there was an inquiry into what damage had been done, and Ingimundr approached his kinsman Guðmundr. The waves had knocked him into the lifeboat and his right foot was hanging over the side so as to be caught in the sail. Ingimundr asked why he didn't stand up. He said that he was so heavy that he couldn't move. Ingimundr asked him why he couldn't get to his feet. He said that his foot was so stiff that he was unable to move at all.

'Do you think it's broken?' asked Ingimundr.

'I don't know,' he said, 'and I have no feeling.'

Then it was looked at and the foot had been broken on the side of the lifeboat into bits and pieces so that the toes pointed in the direction that the heel should have pointed. They tended him there in the boat.

The priest Ingimundr was missing his chest of books, which had been knocked overboard. He felt that very keenly, for his heart was in the books, and the man he loved most was disabled. He thanked God for everything and thought he had quickly solved the dream that he had had the night before, to the effect that he had come to

Archbishop Eysteinn and had been well received. His foster-son interpreted the dream to mean that they would be recipients of a great portent.

The day before they sailed into the breakers Magnús Ámundason spoke up and asked whether they knew where the breakers were that were known as the Þúfa-breakers. They told him that they were off the Strandir. 'I have had a dream that we are close to them.' A little after they had spoken these words, they became aware of the breakers. Now they were driven north to Reykjarfjǫrðr. That was as far as they got, and they furled the sail and cast the anchors overboard. An anchor on a line took hold after a time. They spent the night there. In the morning they got to shore with ship timbers and chopped down their mast and ropes on board and let the ship wash up.

Then it was discussed what to do with Guðmundr. A man who was called Bersi Venison (because one cheek was black as coal) spoke up: 'How will we travel with a broken-footed man since we can't save ourselves—let's pitch him overboard.' Þórarinn rosti answered: 'Spoken like a thoroughgoing wretch, and the right thing would be to fling you overboard, but we will find another solution.' He and Einarr nefja went over the side.

The ship tilted in such a way that the sea was shallow, and they eased Guðmundr down in homespun over the side. Þórarinn and Einarr took hold of him, each holding a leg, and he had an arm around each of their necks. Some men followed them and shielded them against the waves. In this manner they made their way to land though the backwash tried to pull them out. They were able to advance since the surf pushed them forward, and they got to land with him. Then the ship turned away from the land and everything washed out of it. The ship broke into pieces, and not much of the cargo got to shore.

A man lived there whose name was Snorri Arngeirsson. He was a healer. He received Guðmundr, brought him home, and took him in hand to the best of his ability. He had small means but was well disposed.

Many people came from nearby dwellings and wished to lend a hand and help with their losses. The priest Ingimundr made a vow hoping that his book chest and books might make it to shore at Drangar all undamaged; a single clasp was in place and two were broken. All the other chests were broken open, those that reached shore, and everything in them was spilled out. Ingimundr set about drying his books, and he stayed until the feast day of Saint Martin (November 11). Then he went north to meet up with his foster-son, and he was curious to know how his foot was healing. His foot was firm. Then Ingimundr travelled from the north to Breiðabólstaðr in Steingrímsfjǫrðr. Jón Brandsson resided there. He was married to Steinunn, the daughter of Sturla, and [later] to Ingibjǫrg Þorgeirsdóttir, Ingimundr's niece. They gave him a warm reception and he spent the winter there.

When there were three weeks until Easter, Guðmundr came south with his leg bones exposed, and despite that he went south to Breiðabólstaðr on Easter Day (April 5, 1181). His foster-father Ingimundr was happy to see him. He stayed on into Easter week. And then it seemed that his foot could no longer be cared for.

He went south to Reykjahólar on Reykjanes to seek out the priest Helgi Skeljungsson. He was an excellent man and an outstanding healer. He gave Guðmundr a splendid reception, and he stayed there for treatment until the moving days (late May). As soon as he got there, Helgi heated the foot up, and it took two fellows with tongs to loosen the bone before it came out. Then he grew back together, and Guðmundr was healed close to the moving days. After these days he went north to Breiðabólstaðr.

The winter during which he was on the Strandir was called the plague winter. Many men died and were a sore loss: Abbot Bjǫrn at Þverá and Styrkárr the lawspeaker, Oddr Gizurarson, and Arnórr Kolbeinsson. Gizurr Hallsson took over the office of lawspeaker. There was the controversy at Deildartunga. Guðmundr was now twenty years old.

7. Prophetic Words about Bishop Þorlákr

During the following summer Jón Brandsson went north to Þingeyrar for a feast, and Guðmundr Arason went with him because the priest Ingimundr wanted him to go to Háls to stay with Þorvarðr, and that is where he stayed during the winter. Then he was eager to return west to his foster-father, and he went south to the Alþingi with Þorvarðr. That was called the grassless summer.

During that winter the king of Denmark Valdimarr, the son of King Knútr, died. That winter there were also earthquakes, and eleven men perished because of them. At that time Guðmundr was twenty-one years old (1182).

From the Alþingi in the summer he went with Jón Brandsson. That summer Bishop Þorlákr the Saint made his first rounds in the West Fjords. When he arrived in Steingrímsfjǫrðr, he stayed at Kálfanes because there was a new and unconsecrated church there. A fine gathering assembled. Abbot Ǫgmundr was there, and Þorsteinn

Tumason, who later became an abbot. The priest Ingimundr with his foster-son Guðmundr was there.

Guðmundr thought it was more interesting to speak with the bishop's clerics than to attend services or the church consecration. Then the priest Ingimundr spoke to him: 'Go to the services and church consecration and pay close attention because one never knows who will be in line to do such things. I think that the one who needs to learn will never have a better chance to learn from a better man than the one who will perform the office here.'

This was a double prophecy because both parts were later fulfilled, both the words to the effect that Bishop Þorlákr was a truly holy man and that Guðmundr himself would need to perform this office.

In the autumn the priest Ingimundr found a ship in Hvítá and purchased goods for sale and profit, for he was always preparing for travel abroad, as later emerged. The kinsmen parted in Dalir. Sturla procured a following for Guðmundr north to Háls because that is where the priest Ingimundr once more sent him. But he was not comfortable there for more than half a month and then went west and stayed at Breiðabólstaðr during the winter.

8. Guðmundr Charged with a Lawsuit

That winter Guðmundr Bjarnarson at Kleifar in Gilsfjǫrðr was killed. He was a friend of Jón Brandsson's, who persuaded Guðmundr Arason to lead the prosecution. Now Guðmundr summoned Koll-Oddr and brought a case of outlawry. When he was outlawed, Jón Húnrǫðarson took him in. Guðmundr proceeded from the Alþingi west to Saurbœr to execute the confiscation against Oddr at Staðarhóll. From there he went to Breiðabólstaðr to meet his foster-father Ingimundr, and he stayed there as a guest. From there he went to Hvammr to ask his kinsman Sturla to search out his outlaw.

There he learned that Sturla was on his deathbed and he lived only two days after Guðmundr arrived. He stayed there until Sturla was buried. That put an end to the hope he placed in him, but his eagerness was not exhausted. He then put his mind to thinking about how he might pursue his case so that it would not turn into a dishonourable outcome with his being left with an outlaw. Nor did he blame himself for compromising his ordination and ministry. The one who helped and advised him was almighty God, who inspired him to appeal to all-powerful God. He vowed to give all the property that he collected from Oddr's outlawry to God, and that the case should be settled in such a way as not to imperil his soul. Now the story has reached the point where the story of the battle on the heath left off, and the two stories progressed side by side for some time.[1]

9. The Lawsuit is Settled

This year (1183) the case of Hǫgni at Bœr was played out when he married his daughter Snælaug to Þórðr Bǫðvarsson despite two impediments.[2] Bishop Þorlákr the Saint forbade that marriage with such confidence in God that he went to the law rock with his clerical followers and swore an oath that the marriage was contrary to God's

---

[1] The reference here is to the battle on Sælingdalsheiðr described in *Sturlu saga* (note 1 on p. 103 above). The phrasing suggests the knowledge of a written saga, not just a knowledge of the events. *Sturlu saga* is dated in the early thirteenth century and does not provide help on the chronology of these texts.

[2] The story located at Bœr is also told in 'An Account of the People at Oddi' (p. 74 above).

laws. He called witnesses and dissolved the marriage and issued an interdiction against all those who were implicated. That summer five ocean vessels perished and it was known as the summer of maritime losses. During the year Sverrir fought a battle at Íluvellir.[1] At this time Guðmundr was twenty-two years old.

After the death of Sturla, Guðmundr went to Þingeyrar. Þorgrímr alikarl lived there, his friend and foster-brother. He asked Guðmundr to go with him to Vatnsendi in Vestrhóp for a horse match. He answered: 'I don't know how good an idea that is because there will be men there that I don't much care for, my outlaw Oddr and the ones who are shielding him. It tests my patience to see them. But I will nonetheless go if you wish and God will see to it.' They set out accordingly and attended the event.

Jón Húnrǫðarson was there with a big group of ne'er-do-wells, and there was a big stir. Koll-Oddr, the outlaw, was there too. Þórðr Ívarsson from Þorkelshváll was there with a large crowd. Bjarni Hallsson was there, and many men from Miðfjǫrðr along with him. Koll-Oddr and Jón's nephew Húnrǫðr were at odds. They came to blows and Húnrǫðr struck at Oddr, who was wounded on the arm. Jón was angered by this and wanted to strike his kinsman Húnrǫðr. There was much crowding about, and Húnrǫðr struck a second blow at Oddr, but Jón's son, named Eyjólfr, got in the way and was killed. Jón then struck at Þórðr Ívarsson's worker named Þóroddr. A number of other people were wounded.

Now Guðmundr left the gathering after God had taken vengeance against his enemies. Jón lost his son there

---

[1] The battle at Íluvellir took place in 1180 but seems to be misdated to 1183 in this passage.

because of Oddr. But God shielded Guðmundr in such a way that he was involved neither with word or deed. He then went north to the bishop's son Þorgeirr at Staðr and spent the winter with him so well provided for that he later bore witness that no man unrelated to him had treated him as well as Þorgeirr.

The following spring (1184) a case was brought against Jón Húnrǫðarson by Þórðr Ívarsson in the matter of the wound, and Jón was outlawed during the summer. Bishop Brandr and his son Þorgeirr, as well as their kinsmen and friends, supported Þórðr, and they gathered from the north for the confiscation. The conclusion of the matter was that the decision was assigned to Bishop Brandr. The bishop's son Þorgeirr said that no settlement would take effect if it did not include Guðmundr's case of outlawry against Koll-Oddr and the assistance offered him while he was outlawed, and he demonstrated so much affection and good faith toward Guðmundr in this case that there was no other option for settlement. A settlement was reached in this case under the auspices of the bishop and Þorgeirr.

During this year it happened that King Magnús Erlingsson fell at Sogn.[1] At that time Tumi Kolbeinsson died. Then the residences burned at Mǫðruvellir and at Bakki in Miðfjǫrðr. Guðmundr was twenty-three years old.

10. A Voyage to Norway

That summer Guðmundr Arason went to the Alþingi and from there south to Kjarnes to visit with Magnús Ámundason and Þorfinnr, who later became an abbot. With him went the priest Gellir Hǫskuldsson, and therefore he was not present

---

[1] Magnús Erlingsson fell in the Battle of Fimreiti in 1184. See *Sverris saga* (2007), 144.

at the reconciliation meeting at Ásgeirsá.[1] When he had finished his visit there in the south, he went north to Staðr to stay with Þorgeirr and remained there for a year (1185) along with his foster-father, the priest Ingimundr.

In the spring Þorgeirr changed his residence and made ready for a trip abroad; he boarded a ship in Eyjafjǫrðr. That ship belonged to Ǫgmundr rafakollr. He was the father of Helgi who later became bishop in Greenland. The priest Þórálfr Snorrason, Þorsteinn and Þorkell (the sons of Eiríkr), and many other Icelanders embarked with him. That summer (1185) Abbot Karl Jónsson sailed out from Eyjafjǫrðr on another ship together with the priest Ingimundr Þorgeirsson and Ǫgmundr Þorvarðsson and many other Icelanders. There was a man living at Staðr whose name was Hesthǫfði, the son of Guðrún Sæmundardóttir, Bishop Brandr's sister.

The previous winter Einarr Þorgilsson at Staðarhóll died. During that year the party of the Kuflungar came into being.[2] Einarr kati and many good fellows with him perished on All Saints' Day (November 1, 1185). That winter there was a landslide to the east in Geitdalr and eighteen men perished. Guðmundr was now twenty-four years old.

11. Guðmundr's Religious Devotion

That spring during Lent Guðmundr was ordained as a priest by Bishop Brandr four days before Gregory's

---

[1] We have not been told that the reconciliation meeting arranged by Bishop Brandr was held at Ásgeirsá (in Víðidalr). The location here looks like an afterthought.

[2] The Kuflungar were a political party named after their leader Jón kuflungr. *Kuflungr* means 'cowled man', and the name was conferred because Jón had once been a monk. See *Sverris saga* (2007), 155–156.

feast day (March 16, 1185). The priest Ingimundr gave him all his best and most learned books and his priestly garb at parting and took leave of him as a priest in perfect good standing. Then the two men whom he loved most, Ingimundr and Þorgeirr, departed.

The ships now sailed from Eyjafjǫrðr destined for Norway and spent the winter in Trondheim. The bishop's son Þorgeirr spent the winter with Archbishop Eysteinn. The priest Ingimundr was housed and got John's Chapel, attached to Christ Church, for the celebration of Mass. The holidays at Christmas and Easter were celebrated with the archbishop, by whom he was much honoured.

The following spring Þorgeirr went to Iceland with his companions, and the priest Ingimundr stayed behind in Norway. He took over the Church of Mary in Staðr for the celebration of Mass and spent two years there. It is some indication of how highly the archbishop judged his clerical performance that when the first Bishop Jón, known as 'knútr,' died in Greenland, Archbishop Eysteinn wanted to consecrate him as bishop there. But it was a sign of his modesty and caution that he could not be persuaded to do so.

The first winter when the priest Ingimundr was abroad, Guðmundr stayed at Hof with his kinsman Grímr as a priest with a congregation. That winter Bǫðvarr Þórðarson and Þorvarðr the Wealthy died. At that time Guðmundr was twenty-five.

During the summer the bishop's son Þorgeirr became ill at sea and was bedridden until they reached land. His illness grew worse when he landed and he died two days before Saint Mary's earlier feast day (August 13). His body was taken to Hólar and the bishop had no news of his death until they brought the body. This seemed like very bad news to his kinsmen and friends, but most of all to the bishop. Guðmundr Arason said that he had never lost a man whose loss had caused him so much grief. It struck him so hard that you might almost say that he became an altogether different man. He was then staying at Hof.

The priest Guðmundr then became such a devoted man in prayer and holy services and open-handedness and self-mortification that it seemed to some people to border on excess, and they thought he would not be able to bear up under everything, his self-mortification and the death of Þorgeirr.

He brought together aspiring clerics for instruction, and it was his daily routine between services to teach and write. He stayed at church for large parts of the night, both early and late, and he always confessed when he could find a confessor. Wherever he went he learned from the books of everyone such things as he had not known before.

Everyone greatly admired his faith, the wisest people most of all. He included many things in his faith that no other man had included, things that no one had previously aspired to in this country. For another thing, people thought that his character had undergone a great change when he was disabled after the shipwreck off Strandir, for he could endure nothing either day or night until he reached his foster-father. But after that every season saw some improvement in his character. It got to the point that he seemed to have become a wholly different man in his conduct from what the indications suggested when he was young. The same was much in evidence in his blessing of springs and performance of services, which impressed people as highly significant in suggesting that God was pleased with his conduct. It was revealed by most people what they thought of his conduct because he was given a nickname and was called Guðmundr the Good.

But it happened, as is often the case, that not everyone thought the same way, though the intentions were good. Some thanked God as was needful because they had both spiritual and bodily benefit from him, but some were envious because they were less beneficial in important matters than he was. Every year passed in such a way that the whole revenue that he acquired during the winter was expended because he gave it to feed and clothe poor people and his kinsmen. He sustained seven impoverished people in this way.

Now it was attempted by those who envied him to make it more difficult for him and cause him to have less to give for the needs of others by switching congregations and burdening him with the poorer people. Then Bishop Brandr called in the books and vestments at the behest of the men who envied Guðmundr, and the bishop claimed that the church at Hólar was entitled to the inheritance of the priest Ingimundr. But they were unable to erode either his generosity or his self-mortification because the inducement of good men always persuaded him to persist in what he had begun.

Many things happened that year. Jerusalem fell to the Saracens so that all the Christians who were there previously either had to flee or else they were killed, and Christianity was demolished. Darkness covered the sun at midday so that many witless men thought that the end of the world was at hand. That was called the winter of epidemics. There was no grass in the fields and a great famine ensued in the summer. No ship came to Iceland from Norway. Guðmundr was then twenty-six years old.

12. The Icelanders in Norway are Plundered by the King's Guard

In the following spring Guðmundr went to Miklabœr to visit with Bjǫrn, who was known as Affluent Bjǫrn, and he stayed there for two years. The first year he was there (1187) Archbishop Eysteinn died. Before that he had consecrated Jón, foster-son of Sverrir, as the bishop in Greenland. Guðmundr was then twenty-seven years old. The second year King Henry II died in England. That winter Jón, the bishop in Greenland, was in Iceland in the East Fjords.[1] At that time Abbot Ǫgmundr drowned in the spring season, and Abbot Kári died as well.

This year the priest Ingimundr was in Bergen, and his presence was judged all the more notable by wise and outstanding men the better he was known, and he earned great honour from Jón kuflungr and his men. It also happened that Ǫgmundr Þorvarðsson was present and enjoyed great honour. He received his uncle Ingimundr warmly and offered him any assistance he could provide.

The previous spring the priest Ingimundr had made a commercial voyage to England and had returned to Bergen in the autumn. When they came from England with a big supply of wine and honey, wheat and clothing, and many other things, Jón kuflungr's men wanted to help themselves and plunder them. Then Ǫgmundr approached Jón kuflungr and spoke as follows: 'It is true that if King Ingi were alive, he would not allow the brothers of Þorvarðr Þorgeirsson to be plundered if

---

[1] Bishop Jón's visit in the East Fjords was also mentioned in *The Saga of Bishop Páll* (p. 48 above).

they came into his hands, and the same applies to King Magnús because of Ari. Now I might expect of you that for their sake and my appeal you will leave his property in peace.'

Jón answered: 'Quite right, and it will turn out to be true that every penny in his possession will be safe. Proceed yourself, together with your kinsman, and he will be welcome to God and to us.'

Now Ǫgmundr went to the ship and reported Jón's words. Then Jón's men went up to eight large wine casks in the possession of the merchants and asked who owned them. The priest Ingimundr claimed four or five and many other things that they asked about, up to the point where they suspected that he was not as rich as he claimed. They addressed him: 'Now we can see, priest, that you are claiming what other men own, and we are not inclined to lose everything.'

Then they took a cask that turned out to belong to the priest Ingimundr. They also took sixteen ells of homespun reddish in colour that he owned. It was of excellent quality. This he did not want to claim, and he preferred to lose it rather than to have a disagreement.

After that the priest Ingimundr looked for housing and occupied it during the winter. When the winter passed, it happened that he recognised the cloth that had been stolen from him in the autumn, which had been used for the cloaks of the courtiers. He first consulted with Ǫgmundr, telling him to keep it quiet and said that he did not want to be the cause of any trouble, indicating that he was not short of funds. Bjǫrn bríkarnef, the chief of the guards, had arranged the plundering of the priest Ingimundr whereas the courtiers wished to turn over the possessions.

13. The Icelanders Take Revenge and Ingimundr Dies in Greenland

It happened one day that Ǫgmundr caught a glimpse of men wearing the cloaks made of the cloth belonging to the priest Ingimundr, and he told his friends about it, Bárðr sala, Pétr glyfsa, and Eindriði. He said to them: 'Things have come to a bad pass. I saw that Bjǫrn bríkarnef and his companions were walking in the clothes that were stolen from my kinsman, the priest Ingimundr, last autumn.'

Eindriði answered: 'Why did you keep it quiet and not claim them?'

Ǫgmundr answered: 'He himself has no wish to recover them and he wants no trouble to come of it.'

Eindriði replied: 'It should never happen that such evil men trample us under foot and inflict such provocations on our friends. We should surely pursue the matter even if your kinsman has no wish to do so.'

They jump up without delay and go out with axes in hand. The Norwegians went to the drinking hall and Ǫgmundr with them, to the place where Bjǫrn bríkarnef was drinking with his followers, some forty men. Eindriði wanted to go in right away and attack them. But Bárðr said that was not the right approach since there were forty of them while they themselves were only four in number. He asked them to wait until the others came out. It happened by chance that four were chosen to go out and were wearing the suspect clothing. Eindriði immediately struck Bjǫrn a deathblow, and Bárðr and Ǫgmundr and Pétr killed the other three with no defence put up.

Then the guard's trumpet was sounded and almost four hundred men were gathered. The news reached Jón kuflungr and the court trumpet was sounded. Both sides told Jón kuflungr their stories. Bárðr and Pétr were close relatives of Archbishop Eysteinn, and Jón honoured them so greatly in this case that he dismissed the whole body of guards from his service. Qgmundr and the others took possession of the clothing and nothing more was heard of this dispute.

In the following spring the priest Ingimundr prepared to board a ship called Stangarfoli with the destination of Iceland. On board were Bergþórr, the son of Þórðr Ívarsson, and many Icelanders and Norwegians, fine fellows. Their ship landed in the wilderness of Greenland and all the men perished (1189). This was ascertained when fourteen years later their ship was found, and seven men were found in a cave, among them Ingimundr the priest. He was whole and undecayed, and his clothes too, and the bones of six men were next to him. There was wax in the find and runes that told of their death. This seemed to people a strong affirmation of how much the conduct of the priest Ingimundr had pleased God, to wit, how long he was exposed with a whole and intact body.

The summer that Stangarfoli was lost Ásmundr kastanrassi came from Greenland. Now Guðmundr was twenty-eight years old.

14. Miraculous Apparitions

When the priest Guðmundr was at Miklabœr, he celebrated a Mass at the residence called Marbœli. He celebrated it on a feast day. A good and discriminating woman named Hallfríðr Ófeigsdóttir was staying there. She was present at the Mass celebrated by the priest Guðmundr and focused on the Mass as was her custom, and she kept looking at him. When the Gospel was read and he turned aside and said 'Dominus vobiscum', she saw fire coming out of his mouth and up into the air, much brighter than she had seen before. After that he left Miklabœr and went to Víðvík and he stayed there with Már Finnsson for the winter.

It happened once when the priest Guðmundr was in church reciting his prayers, that the farmer Már entered the church. When he got to the church door, he saw a little bird fly up from Guðmundr's shoulder into the air and then disappear.

That year Ásmundr kastanrassi's ship was lost, on which there were many Icelanders who were felt to be a great loss, Abbot Hallr and Jarl Eiríkr.[1] There was a battle to the east in Vík. Now Guðmundr was one year short of thirty.

15. Bishop Þorlákr's Favourites and His Death

In the following spring a woman named Arnþrúðr, who lived at Vellir in Svarfaðardalr, sent word that he should take up residence there under her auspices (1190). She was the daughter of Forni and was his kinswoman. She was a widow. Her husband's name was Eyjólfr, the one she married later on. They had two sons, Brandr and Klœngr. Her previous husband was named Snorri. They had two sons named Þorsteinn and Snorri. But a Norwegian killed her husband Snorri when he refused to pay a debt for a worker, for which he did not have the means. Then Qnundr Þorkelsson took him under his protection and procured passage abroad for him. The cause of their hostility was that the sons of Arnþrúðr were present at the burning of Qnundr.[2]

---

[1] This is Jarl Eiríkr Sigurðarson, a half-brother of King Sverrir.
[2] The burning of Qnundr Þorkelsson is told in *Guðmundar saga dýra,* chapter 14, in *Sturlunga saga* (1946), 187–192; trans. R. George Thomas (1974), II, 180–183.

The next year, when the priest Guðmundr was at Vellir, Sumarliði Ásmundarson was killed at a merchant encampment. That killing was attributed to Snorri Grímsson, Guðmundr's first cousin. Bishop Brandr supported the prosecution brought against Snorri at the Alþingi for intention to kill and complicity with Brandr [Ǫnundarson], who committed the killing. But on the strength of the priest Guðmundr Arason's words and those of many other notable men who supported Snorri, Bishop Þorlákr had the charge of intention to kill dismissed.

Guðmundr was now thirty-one years old. When Guðmundr was two years into his thirties, Bishop Þorlákr the Saint at Skálaholt died two days before Christmas (1193). A short time before he had invited Gizurr Hallsson to stay with him because his state of health had declined. Gizurr was there as long as he lived. Bishop Þorlákr valued three men most greatly, and they were quite unlike any other men. One was his nephew Páll, who was the next bishop after him in Skálaholt, another was Þorvaldr Gizurarson, who became a great chieftain and was more outstanding than his contemporaries, and the third was Guðmundr gríss, who was more devoted to God's service than other men and acted according to the ordinances of the Gospels. On a given day he parted with all his property and loved ones and retired to a monastery.

The son of Guðmundr gríss was Magnús goði, and another was Þorlákr, the father of the first Bishop Árni (1269–1298), one of the most notable men in Iceland. These were the sons of Þorlákr Guðmundarson: the priest Ormr, a canon at Þykkvabœr, and Magnús, who died as a canon at Víðey. Þorlákr's daughters were the nun Ásbjǫrg, the mother of the second Bishop Árni (1304–1320), the abbess Agata, and the sisters Þorgerðr and Guðrún at Kirkjubœr.

Bishop Þorlákr valued all of Gizurr's sons greatly. He fostered Magnús lovingly as long as he wanted to be there. Bishop Þorlákr showed him great honour because he was both wise and learned and very eloquent. Bishop Þorlákr ordained both Þorvaldr and Magnús as priests. Bishop Þorlákr also provided living quarters for his nephew Ormr Jónsson at Breiðabólstaðr in Fljótshlíð, the residence that seemed to him best of those he managed.

The summer after Bishop Þorlákr had died during the winter, Snorri Þórðarson from the West Fjords died on the feast day of Remigius.[1]

16. Guðmundr Defends the Legitimacy of Relics

Now it can be told about the priest Guðmundr Arason that when he had been at Vellir a few years and the lady of the house Arnþrúðr had gone to Sakka in Svarfaðardalr with her sons Brandr and Klœngr, it happened one summer at the Alþingi that the abbess Halldóra, daughter of Eyjólfr, from Kirkjubœr invited the priest Guðmundr to move east with her in the capacity of a manager. He agreed to this, and she was to send men to meet him in the summer.

After the feast day of Saint Óláfr (July 29) a ship came to Gásir with Bishop Páll on board. Then Bishop Brandr rode to Grund and met with Bishop Páll there. The priest Guðmundr also came. He took leave of the bishops and went on to Kirkjubœr. When the men of the district learned this, they sought out Bishop Brandr and asked him to forbid the priest Guðmundr to move away. This he did. When they met up with the priest Guðmundr and told

---

[1] There is more than one Remigius, but this one may be Saint Remigius of Reims, who lived in the fifth and early sixth century in what is now France. There is a *Remigius saga*, ed. C. R. Unger (1877), II, 222–227.

him what the bishop had said, he immediately went to see the bishop. The bishop said that he forbade him to move away. Guðmundr then rode to Vellir and spent the winter there. Bishop Brandr valued this event so highly that he thought it analogous to the story of Pope Gregory.[1]

During the following winter there was discord between the priest Guðmundr and Þorsteinn Þraslaugarson, who lived at Vellir, because the men of the district turned over money to Guðmundr that they had committed to holy men, and Þorsteinn claimed that Guðmundr took the money. It was the custom of the priest Guðmundr to let people kiss holy relics on holidays, but Þorsteinn said that he did not know whether these were the bones of holy men or horses' bones. This placed them at loggerheads to the point where Þorsteinn sought out Bishop Brandr, asking him to get rid of the priest Guðmundr. The following spring Bishop Brandr went north to Vellir and learned from all the district men there in the north that they on no account wished to be rid of Guðmundr. The bishop offered him a church position in Vellir, but he was not inclined. Then the bishop moved another priest into that position.

The priest Guðmundr issued two summonses against Þorsteinn in the spring, one concerning the fact that he had accused him of stealing charitable funds and the other concerning blasphemy occasioned by his calling the bones of holy men horses' bones. On the moving days he moved away to Ufsir. In the summer Guðmundr rode to the Alþingi, and in his cases he was given self-judgment.

From the Alþingi Sigurðr Ormsson invited him to Svínafell. He proceeded south to Haukadalr and then east

---

[1] Perhaps this refers to the legend that Pope Gregory wished to escape his papal duties. See the first sentence of his *Pastoral Care* (1978), 20, and Frederick H. Dudden, *Gregory the Great* (1905), I, 225–228.

to Svínafell, and from there to the East Fjords and on to the district of Fljótsdalr, then Vápnafjǫrðr and Øxarfjǫrðr and finally from the north down to Eyjafjǫrðr and home to Ufsir around midwinter. On his itinerary a number of notable things occurred that I could tell of with respect to services and the blessing of water.

17. Guðmundr's Role in the Sanctification of Bishop Þorlákr

That same spring when, in the following autumn, the sons of Þórðr and Arnþrúðr were killed at Laufás, the priest Guðmundr Arason went to stay at Staðr in Skagafjǫrðr, since Kolbeinn Arnórsson invited him there.

After the Alþingi Bishop Páll sent men from the south for Bishop Brandr and the priest Guðmundr Arason, telling them to come south to Skálaholt right after the Alþingi to raise Bishop Þorlákr's relics from the earth. They set out after the Alþingi and arrived at Skálaholt on the feast day of Margrét (July 20, 1198). In the service that was performed for the glory of God and blessed Þorlákr, Bishop Páll placed Guðmundr Arason next to the bishops for the whole service, and they permitted him to dry off the casket with them when it was carried into the church. He also had an important say in what was sung when the holy relic was raised. There were many miracles testifying to the honour of blessed Bishop Þorlákr.

18. Guðmundr's Travels and Role in the Sanctification of Bishop Jón

After this the priest Guðmundr went home and stayed at Staðr with Kolbeinn that year. But in the spring he moved to Víðimýrr with Kolbeinn Tumason (1199). That summer the priest Guðmundr went to the Alþingi and from the Alþingi west to Borgarfjǫrðr; many men all over the district invited him. From there he went west to Hvammr and attended Snorri Sturluson's wedding feast. Thereafter he went to Fagradalr and from there to Reykjahólar, where he blessed the spring that they later urinated in to mock him, but the water nonetheless became better than before. From there he travelled to Steingrímsfjǫrðr and on to Miðfjǫrðr, then home to Víðimýrr in the autumn, and he was held in high regard there during the winter. Kolbeinn considered him with such honour and affection that he called him a truly saintly man. He said that he himself had experienced many proofs of it. During the previous summer a feast day for Bishop Þorlákr was legally adopted.

That winter, while the priest Guðmundr was at Víðimýrr, there was stormy weather, and it was hard on many people. There were dreams about the sanctity of Bishop Jón, to the effect that he revealed that the weather would improve if his holy relics were exhumed.[1] This was put into effect by Bishop Brandr, and he sent word to the priest Guðmundr Arason that he should come and be in charge of this rite because the bishop himself was confined to bed. The bishop summoned men, but the weather was so harsh that the priest Guðmundr came a day later than appointed. They nonetheless waited for him. When he arrived, the holy relics of Bishop Jón were exhumed and attested by many miracles seven days after the feast day of Saint Matthew (September 21, 1200). In the spring the priest Guðmundr went north to Eyjafjǫrðr. While he was away from home, his mother Úlfheiðr died, and her body

---

[1] Bishop Jón's remains were exhumed in March of 1200.

was brought to Hólar, where the bishop affectionately received it. Now the priest Guðmundr returned, and then left home again. He went to the Alþingi in the summer. The feast day for Bishop Jón was legally adopted at the request of Bishop Brandr and on the strength of a speech by the priest Guðmundr at the legislature.

From the Alþingi the people from the West Fjords invited him. He went first to Borgarfjǫrðr and from there to Breiðafjǫrðr. From Reykjanes he was transported to Flatey. Þorgils Gunnsteinsson had his son and one worker transport the priest Guðmundr. He asked the priest Guðmundr to give his companions a good breeze when they returned 'because they are not strong,' he said, 'and I commend them into your hands.' 'I will ask God,' said the priest, 'that he give them a good breeze.'

The sea was becalmed when they got to Flatey. The companions prepared to leave and went to the ship to set sail. They asked the priest to fulfill his undertaking concerning the breeze. He went to the church. And when they were ready, they raised the sail and the wind sprang up behind them; they did not lower the sail until they got home, and the breeze got better and better the longer they sailed.

19. Guðmundr's Further Travels and Miraculous Interventions

Now the priest Guðmundr went to the West Fjords. When he was in Sauðlausdalr, he blessed the water that a woman brought home in her hood. From there he went to the northern fjords as far as Keldudalr, to the home of Þórðr Arason. He had a withered hand with such pain that he could not cut his own food. At night when he thought he could not lie still, he would go out. When he came in, he saw a great light shining from the priest Guðmundr's bed, as if a beam were shining from above. He stretched his crippled hand into the light, and the light shining on his hand was as bright as ever. After that the hand was healthy and free of pain, and the light was extinguished.

From there he went to Haukadalr to the home of Árni rauðskeggr. In the evening when he went to bed, a woman was there to scratch his foot. Her hand was misshapen so that the fingers curled into the palm. When it seemed to him that the scratching was too gentle, he kicked out hard with his foot and his heel struck into the hollow of her hand where the fingers were curled, so that she was somewhat hurt. A few nights later she came to see him and showed him her healed hand. All those who saw this thanked God.

Then he proceeded to Ísafjǫrðr and arrived at Súðavík on the feast day of Saint Matthew (September 21).[1] There he gave the value of thirty hundreds to his kinsman Bárðr as a bride price, who was then betrothed to the daughter of the priest Steinþórr Bjarnarson.

Subsequently a woman named Þuríðr came running up. She had kept company with Árni rauðskeggr despite Bishop Páll's interdiction, and he could not separate them. But when she learned of the teachings of the priest Guðmundr, she was eager for nothing as much as meeting him. She had to be hidden from Árni because he was infatuated with her, and they had children together. She was also beautiful in appearance. She now came to the priest Guðmundr on the feast day of Saint Matthew and begged him with tears of repentance for mercy and

---

[1] Súðavík is on the southern coast of Ísafjǫrðr in the West Fjords.

refuge so that she might be free of her difficulties. She received such grace from her meeting with him that she never returned to the same difficulties and stayed in his [Guðmundr's] company constantly thereafter when they were not separated by contending factions.

From there he went to Vatnsfjǫrðr and on to Steingríms-fjǫrðr to the home of Jón Brandsson, and he was accompanied by many men. It was said that men were sent to let people know in advance and so that they did not arrive unexpectedly. But the priest Guðmundr said that it was not necessary—'and God will provide for us and send a whale before we leave.' These words were fulfilled, and on the very same day a whale was stranded on Jón's shore, which was his alone, and the stranding of the whale was reported the next morning. Jón gave the priest Guðmundr a book that was a treasure and which Bishop Páll had given Jón. From there he travelled to Broddanes and then north across the bay to Miðfjǫrðr and on to Vatnsdalr.

When he was at Hof that autumn, it happened that he sang over a bedridden man and displayed his holy relics over him. He lay on the bench by the sick man and fell asleep in the midst of prayer, or so it seemed to those present. His deacon lay on a bench next to him and the priest Guðmundr turned over on him as he slept. When he had lain there a short time, the deacon perceived no weight, but others saw that he was lying there. That lasted for a very long time. When he woke up, the deacon asked why he did not feel his weight while he lay on top of him. But he did not wish to say.

Then a report came from the western fjords that a man named Snorri to the west in Skálavík was the victim of a certain witch who so beleaguered him that he thought there was no escape. During the night previously mentioned (it was a Saturday night) Snorri went to services by himself and had a long way to go. The troll woman came at him and attacked him and chased him into the mountains. Then he implored the priest Guðmundr to help him, if he was so empowered by God as he thought, and free him from the witch. Then it seemed to him as if a light came over him, and a man in a clerical robe and holding an aspergil in his hand sprinkled it on her. Then the troll woman vanished as if sinking into the earth. But the light followed him all the way to his residence. He seemed to recognise clearly that the priest Guðmundr Arason followed the light.

Now the two things coincided so that at one and the same time Snorri had a revelation and the deacon felt no weight from Guðmundr's body. That same deacon had a swelling on his head. One time as he stood below the priest Guðmundr at Mass, the latter's elbow rested on the swelling, and it was very sore. But when the Mass was over, he perceived no soreness from the swelling.

Then they went to Þingeyrar and arrived there before All Saints' Day (November 1, 1200). Abbot Karl and the monk Gunnlaugr were there.[1] They processed toward him during the day, and he was a priest at that time.[2] They sang the following responsorium to greet him: 'Vir iste in populo suo mitissimus apparuit sanctitate dei et gratia

---

[1] Karl Jónsson and Gunnlaugr Leifsson at the monastery of Þingeyrar were important figures in early Icelandic literature. Karl Jónsson was the author of at least part and conceivably the whole of *Sverris saga*. Gunnlaugr wrote a saga about Óláfr Tryggvason and a version of *Jóns saga helga*, and translated Geoffrey of Monmouth's *Prophecies of Merlin*.

[2] The meaning is perhaps that he was not yet a bishop, so that there was no obvious reason to accord him so much honour.

plenus; iste est, qui assidue . . .' This all combines to show how much men honoured his counsel before they became blind with arrogance. Then he preached at length on All Saints' Day.

From there he went out to Blǫndubakki and spent a long time there. Next he was transported up along Langadalr, and men were sent after the horse that was the stoutest and strongest in the valleys, though they were refused. But during the night the horse fell into the home water supply and died. Now the priest Guðmundr travelled on until he got to Víðimýrr on the feast day of Saint Nicholas (December 6, 1200). Kolbeinn was completely delighted. He [Guðmundr] was there at home during the winter and was held in high regard.

20. Guðmundr Celebrates the Nun Ketilbjǫrg and Performs Further Miracles

In the spring he accepted invitations in the northern parts of the district around Eyjafjǫrðr and on Flatey and to the north of the Alþingi. Then he rode to the Alþingi. Many people issued invitations from the Alþingi, southerners and easterners. One night when he was there, the nun Ketilbjǫrg died. Bishop Páll asked the priest Guðmundr to sing over her body, and the bishop and Gizurr Hallsson stood with him. That service was so notable that Gizurr testified in his oration over her grave that they felt they had never heard such a funerary dirge, and he accounted her holy because such a performance was granted her.

From there he crossed the rivers to the east. Then the priest Árni at Skúmsstaðir invited him home. There was a major epidemic so that seven people had perished, as well as both beasts and horses. He stayed as a guest there and blessed water and circulated with holy relics. He personally sprinkled water over the fields and the home yard and widely over the grazing land. The epidemic immediately came to an end.

From there he went east to Eyjafjǫll and farther east to Síða and Ver. He came then to the residence called Lómagnúpr. There was such a rush in the river that the landowner Árni had barely escaped, and one of his men died in the onslaught of the river. It caused havoc over wide stretches of the land. People were located to the east of the river and could not get across because the river was plainly untraversable. When the priest Guðmundr and his companions came to the river, they dismounted and saw that the river could not be crossed, but they waited. Then they saw that the water level was falling. When they had sat a long time by the river without daring to ride into it, those who sat on the east bank saw that the level was falling and decided to ride into it. Then the priest Guðmundr and his companions also rode into the river, and they met near the midpoint, they themselves and the ones from the east. Both fared well. When both groups had got over the river, it immediately became swollen again and was impassable for a few days after that.

21. Guðmundr Visits with Sigurðr Ormsson at Svínafell

From there the priest Guðmundr travelled to Sigurðr Ormsson at Svínafell. Kolbeinn Tumason had come there for a stay, and the three of them were all together there for three days. Then Kolbeinn rode away, and Sigurðr and Guðmundr accompanied him part of the way. When they parted, the priest Guðmundr and Sigurðr rode alone together because Sigurðr wanted to discuss his problems with Guðmundr privately, problems stemming from his differences with Sæmundr Jónsson, and he said that he could scarcely endure the injury and blame growing out of their dispute.[1] He sought the counsel of the priest Guðmundr, and he said that nothing was more important to him than taking revenge against Sæmundr.

The priest Guðmundr urged him most of all to be cautious—'for you must live with being reproached for having done good. Now I will entreat God to strengthen and protect you.'

'What I ask of you,' said Sigurðr, 'is that you ask God to enable you to procure for me a residence in the northern districts with a measure of honour, for I think so highly of you that I am inclined to believe that you will have even greater authority than now. And I would like to transfer this residence into the hands of my kinsman Jón Sigmundarson. Now I will either relent, providing you will give me your promise, or I will try my luck with Sæmundr, no matter how it turns out.' The priest Guðmundr said that he would rather promise to ask God to let him prevail in this matter.

The very day that they discussed this Bishop Brandr died (August 6, 1201). The words of both turned out to be true, the words about the promising appearance that Sigurðr thought he detected in Guðmundr and the willing promise that the priest gave Sigurðr if he could put an end to his dissension with Sæmundr and acquire a property for him. On that day the governance of the bishopric devolved on him, though they did not know it.

---

[1] There is further information on this dispute in *Íslendinga saga*. See p. 92 n. 2 above.

22. Guðmundr again Defends Relics and Takes Leave of a Dying Woman

It came about then that Sigurðr asked the priest Guðmundr to give him holy relics, and he did so. When he gave him something of the bones of Bishop Jón, a priest named Steinn said that he thought that the bone was discoloured and less than holy. The priest Guðmundr answered softly and asked whether he believed Bishop Martin to be less holy because his bones were dusky and whether he thought Bishop Þorlákr holy or not. The priest Steinn answered and said that he thought that Bishop Jón was no more than half the stature of Bishop Þorlákr. The priest Guðmundr then spoke: 'Now let us all ask God and Saint Jón the bishop to reveal his holiness with some sign to counteract the disbelief of the priest Steinn.' Then all fell on their knees with the priest Guðmundr. After that he had everyone kiss the bone. All of them smelled a great fragrance from the bone as if from the sweetest incense, all except the priest Steinn, who detected no fragrance.

Then the priest Steinn was ashamed of his disbelief and his own words, and he understood the wrath of God and Bishop Jón against him since he was not included in this glorious event, and he entreated God and Bishop Jón the Saint with tears for forgiveness.

Now the priest Guðmundr offered to share the bone of Bishop Jón if he would only worship him with all his heart. He said he was eager to do so but was afraid that Bishop Jón the Saint would not accept his worship. Then the priest Guðmundr said that everyone should ask that Bishop Jón the Saint should grant the priest Steinn forgiveness for his words. When Steinn took hold of the bone, he perceived the same fragrance as others. Then everyone thanked God and Bishop Jón the Saint. All the bells were rung and Te Deum was sung, and in this way the miracle was made public.

Another event occurred there, the flooding of the river that runs next to the residence, which washed away fields and home field so that great damage was done. Then Sigurðr asked the priest Guðmundr to approach and sing over the river. He proceeded with holy relics and a following of clerics and sang over the river for a long time. The next morning it had left its channel and created a new channel from the east over the sands.

An old woman was bedridden at Svínafell and so close to death that she had not spoken a word for seven days and had tasted no food and had flexed nothing except the ends of her fingers and toes. But she still breathed. All the last rites had been administered to her. She was a fine person.

When the priest Guðmundr was ready to leave Svínafell and had got to his horse, he said: 'It is a fact,' he said, 'that I have not kissed the blessed old woman who is sick. I should not leave it at that.' Then he went in, and a whole group of people with him. He went into the living area where the old woman lay, and people thought she was near death. He kissed her and said: 'Farewell, dear woman; now you will pass on to God. Give my greetings to Mary, mother of God, and to the archangel Michael, and John the Baptist, and Peter and Paul, and to King Óláfr, and especially to Saint Ambrose, to whom I am devoted.' The old woman answered so clearly that the people outside the room heard it equally well. 'Yes,' said the old woman. That was the last word she spoke. It was close to noon and she died in the mid-afternoon of the same day.

23. Guðmundr is Nominated as Bishop

Then the priest Guðmundr and his company went to the East Fjords and arrived at Stafafell on the feast day of Saint Bartholomew (August 24). There he learned at matins of the death of Bishop Brandr Sæmundarson. At this news he was startled as if he had been struck by a stone. He immediately arranged for a requiem to be sung and a funeral dirge with all meticulousness and affection.

Then they set out and came to the district of Fljótsdalr and to Valþjófsstaðir and arrived at the residence of Jón Sigmundarson on the feast day of Efidius (September 1). That was a church anniversary day, and they were well received. When Jón led the priest Guðmundr into the church in the evening, Guðmundr asked him for news. Jón told of great and good news: 'The men of Skagafjǫrðr will meet tomorrow and choose a bishop, and you will be chosen because that is God's wish.' From that time on Guðmundr felt such great apprehension in his heart that he could neither sleep nor eat with comfort because of his fear and alarm at such a prospect.

On the evening before the Exaltation of the Cross (September 13) the priest Guðmundr came to the residence called Hlíð in the district of Fljótsdalr. At night he dreamed that he was coming into the church at Vellir in Svarfaðardalr, and it seemed to him that the altar was falling into his arms and was decorated with the greatest ornamentation.

The following day they travelled north across the heath to Vápnafjǫrðr and arrived at Krossavík in the evening. When they were at table, messengers came from Kolbeinn Tumason, and Einarr Fork went ahead to the priest Guðmundr and gave him a warm greeting. Guðmundr asked for news. Einarr said: 'The news is good. You have been chosen as bishop by Kolbeinn and all the men of the district. Now I am coming with letters and the message that you should return home as quickly as possible.' At this news he was so startled that he could not say a word for a long time. Then he asked God to let whatever happen that was best for everybody.

24. Guðmundr Tries to Elude his Nomination

The following day the priest Guðmundr went to the residence of Teitr Oddsson at Hof. The priest Halldórr Hallvarðsson was staying there. Guðmundr consulted Halldórr on whether there was any chance that he might extricate him from his difficulty and assume it himself. He declined and said that he had grown very old and was in other respects not qualified. He said that he was convinced that it would do no good to beg off: 'It is no doubt the wish of both God and men that you should become bishop. But I will assist you with my prayers and do everything in my power to support you.'

From there Guðmundr went north to Øxarfjǫrðr and Mǫðrudalsheiðr, and they encountered a great blustering storm and a heavy snowfall. Their company was split up until the priest Guðmundr realised that they were probably not on the right track. He was the first to get to a house, and two deacons with him, Sturla Bárðarson and Lambkárr Þorgilsson, but others got there much later.

Now they travelled south and came to Grenjaðarstaðir. Eyjólfr Hallsson was living there at the time. Then the priest Guðmundr addressed Eyjólfr, asking if he would agree to become the bishop. He said not to put that question and that the men of Skagafjǫrðr and Eyjafjǫrðr wanted none other than Guðmundr.

Now they went south and came to Háls, the residence of Ǫgmundr Þorvarðsson. Ǫgmundr asked whether it was true that he was trying to avoid being bishop. He said that it was so. 'What is the cause?' said Ǫgmundr. He answered: 'Because it seems to me very difficult to deal with many disobedient, envious, and powerful men. Or, kinsman, will you be submissive if we are critical of your situation?'

Ǫgmundr answered: 'For whose difficulties will you be more responsible than for mine? To the extent that I am disobedient toward you, I will be even more disobedient to all others, and it will do no good for others to find fault. Nor will it do any good for you to excuse yourself, for you will have the same lot as Bishop Ambrose just as your childhood games predicted for you as for him that you would become a bishop.[1] It did him no good to find excuses and that will apply to you too. We want no other bishop than you.' Now the priest Guðmundr went home west in Víðimýrr in midwinter, and everyone was delighted at his return home.

25. Pressure Brought to Bear on Guðmundr

That Saturday Þorvarðr Þorgeirsson went to speak to the priest Guðmundr alone. He asked whether it was true that he wanted to become isolated by talking his way out of the consecration as bishop and not adhering to his own counsel and that of other wise men. He said that was

---

[1] Perhaps this refers to an anecdote at the beginning of the *Life of Saint Ambrose* according to which honeybees buzz about his mouth as he sleeps in a cradle—an anticipation of his honeyed words in later life. This is hardly a game, but a prophetic moment in childhood. See '*Ambrosius saga byskups*' in *Heilagra manna søgur* (1877), I, 29.

true. 'I think,' said Þorvarðr, 'that I am entitled to be your supervisor, and I wish to decide.'

Guðmundr said: 'How can it be that it is not up to me to decide for myself?'

Then Þorvarðr said: 'You know, kinsman, that I have been the chieftain in our family and my father before me. Your father abided by my instructions and other of my kinsmen as well. This is the counsel I give you. Then the chieftainship will devolve on you after me.'

Guðmundr said: 'You did not offer that I should inherit property from my father, and you have done little to promote my honour apart from having me beaten to book learning.[1] Indeed it seems to me that you prefer to make trouble for me rather than honour, and I will not agree to this.'

Þorvarðr answered: 'When have I ever heard of rejecting one's own honour? Nor will it do any good because you will become the bishop, and that is a dream I have had.'

'What did you dream?' asked Guðmundr.

'I dreamed that I was going into a large house with a high ceiling, and I had never seen one so large and with such wide doors that they were hardly smaller than the house. When my head had got into the doorway, my shoulders got stuck and I could get no farther. I interpret the dream to mean that your honour will be so great that the whole of Christendom will not be able to compass the extent of your honour. Then I had a second dream in which I seemed to be going north to Trondheim and into the hall of King Óláfr, and I seemed to see him sitting on his throne with his hall in full

---

[1] Guðmundr's early distaste for book learning seems to have remained a haunting memory. See pp. xxxix and 101 above.

session. I seemed to see him stand up to greet me and open his arms and address me: 'You are very welcome, Þorvarðr, and you will be blessed in all the northern lands.' Now I know that you are the subject of these dreams. God grant that you should be consecrated in the hall of Saint Óláfr, that is, in Christ Church, where you will be consecrated as bishop, and that will happen whether you wish it or not.'

Then they parted, and Þorvarðr told Kolbeinn of their conversation. Kolbeinn went to see Guðmundr and said that they had had a meeting on the feast day of Egidius at Vellir [Víðivellir in Skagafjǫrðr] (September 1). 'Present at the meeting were the abbots from Þingeyrar and Þverá, and present were Gizurr Hallsson and Guðmundr inn dýri and many men from the district. You and Magnús Gizurarson were nominated, and Gizurr made the case for his son, and there seemed to be more help and support from him, and more financial experience in his case than yours. I said I was well pleased with the election of either of you. Then Hjálmr Ásbjarnarson and Hafr and many others said that they were not interested in having someone elected from some other quarter. Everyone was so much in agreement that there was no opposition, and everyone was in accord. And now you are firmly elected as the choice of God and men. Now we expect that you will conform both to God's will and ours and not withdraw from consideration.'

He answered: 'I would like to know and be told whether the other men of the district are in accord with you, for it seems to me that great difficulty is involved and I am therefore reluctant to agree.'

26. Guðmundr Acquiesces but Anticipates Trouble

A meeting was convened on a Sunday at Víðimýrr, and the men of the district gathered and opened the discussion anew. The outcome was the same. They sent for the priest Guðmundr, and Kolbeinn told him that they asked for his consent and a positive response so that he might undertake the difficult task, to which they had elected him, and become bishop.

When the priest Guðmundr saw what view Kolbeinn took of the matter and that he would hear of nothing else, he thought that might be the easiest way out. Then he answered: 'I would rather take a chance with God's mercy and agree to this trial than to run the risk that no one is elected.' Then Kolbeinn answered: 'A blessing on you for your response.' And now everyone thanked him anew and they returned home in the evening.

In the evening a high-seat was prepared for him, and Kolbeinn served him himself and spread a cloth on the table. Because there was not much time, the cloth was very tattered, and Kolbeinn commented on it: 'We are making things easy for ourselves rather than honouring you when such a wretched cloth is spread on your table.' He answered: 'The cloth is of no concern. But my episcopacy may follow suit and be tattered like the cloth.' Kolbeinn turned red and said nothing.

The next morning they prepared to go to Hólar with the candidate for bishop together with Kolbeinn and Þorvarðr and Guðmundr's own clerics. Kolbeinn presented him with a full-grown ox in the morning and said that he would be the first to give him gifts. He gave him warm thanks. Then they proceeded to Hólar during the day and arrived on the evening of the day before the feast day of the virgins of Cologne.[1] A procession came to meet him.

When they arrived there, Kolbeinn took all the resources under his control, including the household management, without consulting the candidate for bishop. Kygri-Bjǫrn was present at Hólar. Before they got to Hólar, the deacon Lambkárr had always attended to the documents when Guðmundr was at home. But as soon as he got to Hólar, he was shunned in all secretarial matters and Kygri-Bjǫrn was put in charge of the documentation in his place. Kolbeinn was on closer terms with Bjǫrn than with anyone. But Bjǫrn was immediately in opposition to the candidate for bishop because he thought himself too little honoured by him. He right away predicted what later came to pass concerning Bjǫrn because an enmity developed between them that became more acute the longer it continued.

As the winter advanced, Kolbeinn took charge of everything, and the candidate for bishop was so overshadowed that he could not get his nephews to live there and provided a home for them at Kálfstaðir with his summer income. But Kolbeinn allowed himself to settle in on the church property with six others. The candidate for bishop wanted the poor people to be given two meals, but Kolbeinn shunted them off into the guest buildings and had them provided with a single meal.

When Christmas passed, Þórarinn the Steward arrived on the evening of Epiphany (January 13, 1202) to speak with the candidate for bishop. He said the following: 'You are not curious about the house management that we have appropriated.' Guðmundr replied: 'It doesn't seem to me the best option to get involved and have nothing to say.'

[1] On the 11,000 virgins of Cologne see p. 99 n. 1 above.

Þórarinn said: 'I will still tell you the situation. I have put in such provisions for Christmas as is customary. Every previous winter there has been a scrimping of Christmas provisions, and now it has gone on a week longer, although there has never been a bigger crowd for Christmas than now.'

'It is clear,' said Guðmundr, 'that Saint Mary likes provisioning better than Kolbeinn.' Kolbeinn was sitting there and was silent. Then the steward went away.

Next the herdsman came in and said that the cattle feed on hand had never been as plentiful as now. The candidate for bishop answered in the same vein: 'Who knows whether Saint Mary is not more pleased with provisioning than Kolbeinn?'

27. Tensions with Kolbeinn and Final Acquiescence

After Christmas the candidate for bishop sent a man named Þórðr Vermundarson to summon Hrafn Sveinbjarnarson to a meeting with him in Miðfjǫrðr. The candidate for bishop had it in mind to ask him to join him in a passage abroad. When the time came, the candidate for bishop prepared to set out from home. When he had got into his cart, Kolbeinn went up to him and spoke to him: 'I hope now that we can put aside the conflict that we have had during the winter, for that is the only problem, and we should not hold it against one another.'

The candidate for bishop answered: 'I think I have done no wrong. It is a good thing if you have done wrong and take responsibility yourself if matters are not as you wish.'

Kolbeinn answered: 'Neither of us is the sole cause, as is often the case. Now it is more likely that we are more at fault. For that reason we wish to ask you for forgiveness. And we wish to forgive you if you have committed wrong in any way.'

He answered: 'Good words are a good thing, and both of us probably fail to recognise our deeds, for I am unaware that I have been guilty of any wrong this winter; I have had no options.'

Now he went to the western districts and stayed over at Þingeyrar. A good and intelligent nun lived there, an anchorite named Úlfrún. She was the mother of the priest Big Símon. She was such a devout anchorite that she did not wish to see her son when he visited her. She told the candidate for bishop that Mary had revealed to her that God and she wished him to be bishop—'and therefore you should not remove yourself from consideration if you wish to do God's will, as I am sure you do, because that is foreordained.' This utterance seemed important to him, and he had confidence in it.

He then went to Miðfjǫrðr and came to Staðarbakki on a given day. That same evening Hrafn Sveinbjarnarson came from the West Fjords as was agreed. The candidate for bishop delivered a long and remarkable sermon on Sunday and announced that if any man who had come there would agree, or knew of anyone who would assume the difficult position for which he was destined, or anyone who wished to replace him—'then I will happily defer if that is in accordance with people's wishes.' But nobody had the confidence to replace him. At that meeting the passage abroad of the candidate for bishop and Hrafn Sveinbjarnarson was arranged. From that meeting both of them returned home, the candidate for bishop north to Hólar and Hrafn to the West Fjords.

28. Exchanges of Letters and Guðmundr's Consecration

In the winter the candidate for bishop sent a man to deliver a letter east at Svínafell. It read as follows:

> Guðmundr, who is now called the candidate for bishop, sends God's greeting and his own to Sigurðr and Þuríðr. God has performed great miracles so that we might fulfill our promise as we owe it to you, that is, to procure a residence for you. Now I am in need of your help since I have agreed to a more difficult mission than I am able to perform. Now I offer you to become estate managers and treasurers for me, and come at your earliest convenience because that is most beneficial for the church estate and all of us. Farewell.

Now Sigurðr travelled from the east after Christmas, and he and the candidate for bishop met en route as Sigurðr headed north. Sigurðr proceeded more speedily north to Hólar.

When the candidate for bishop came to Hólar, it was discussed what terms Sigurðr should have. He said that he did not want to assume the task unless the church management were turned over to him. The candidate for bishop was reluctant to turn it over, but he said he would put the church management in Sigurðr's hands.

At that time wise men like Kolbeinn Tumason and Hafr Brandsson and many others advised that the candidate for bishop should rather entrust matters of the church estate to Sigurðr than to dismiss such a man as Sigurðr was, and people judged that no better provision could be made for the church estate than to confer it on Sigurðr and Þuríðr. The final decision was that he appointed Sigurðr joint custodian of the church estate with himself.

Then Sigurðr went with a letter from the candidate for bishop to Skálaholt to deliver to Bishop Páll. It was worded as follows:

> The priest Guðmundr, now referred to as the candidate for bishop, sends God's greetings and his own to Bishop Páll. I have agreed to more difficulty than I am able to undertake and have not had your counsel or leave as I should have. Now I wish to ask you to consider what is closest to your heart. If you wish to select another man for this honour and arduous task, which I am unworthy to agree to, I will gladly relinquish it and withdraw, for I have become aware from what people say that it seems I have overreached. I have appointed Sigurðr Ormsson as co-manager with me since people were apprehensive about my managerial skills. Now make a quick choice whether to designate me or not, as God counsels you, and send me a letter as soon as you can. Farewell.

When Sigurðr brought Bishop Páll this letter, he sent a man east to Sæmundr in Oddi with a letter:

> Bishop Páll sends God's greetings and his own to his brother Sæmundr. A letter from the candidate for bishop has come to me saying that I should choose another man as a bishop if I wish. He says that he is willing to forego his election. He has appointed Sigurðr Ormsson as manager because people were afraid that his managerial skills would not be adequate. I think I can detect from his letter that he intends to go abroad in the summer if he is not rejected, for he has asked me to make a quick

choice whether I wanted to choose him or not. Now I want you to tell me how I should respond.

Sæmundr sent a letter in reply and wrote as follows:

> Sæmundr sends God's greeting and his own to Bishop Páll. You know, brother, that the candidate for bishop has not been a good friend in our contention with Sigurðr [Ormsson]. But still he is much praised by people and therefore the choice is likely to fall on him for the reason that this is God's will. I have learned that in many respects he is well qualified both because of his goodness and austerity and chaste life, which is of the greatest importance. If there are other considerations, then relieve the northerners of their burden so that they may assume the responsibility for their own choice. It is my advice that you should rather choose than reject him, for it is not certain who is more likely to please God better than this man, and it is best to take a chance on what is most promising; it is unlikely that a man can be identified in whom no fault is found. The northerners will be wilful about their choice. Let them have the responsibility for how it turns out.

Now the letter arrived at Skálaholt. The bishop sent word to Þorvaldr Gizurarson and Hallr and his brother Magnús and to Sigurðr Ormsson. They gathered for a meeting. The bishop announced that the choice had been left up to him and that he was determined to choose Guðmundr as bishop and not reject him. They all formally committed themselves to this. The bishop [and Sigurðr sent Ingimundr Grímsson] north with letters to the candidate for bishop Guðmundr with these words:

Bishop Páll sends God's greeting and his own to the candidate for bishop Guðmundr. God and we have chosen you as bishop, and you are firmly elected by the laws of God and men as fully as possible in this country. Now that God and good men have laid this burden on you, it is needful to meet with you as soon as possible, for I have detected from your letter that you intend to sail abroad this summer if the choice is up to you. I wish now to meet you at your convenience or would be grateful if you visited me at home but place you under no obligation, for I have many pressing matters for the archbishop that make me wish to meet with you before you go abroad. Farewell.

Now winter passes. After the week of Pentecost the candidate for bishop went south to Skálaholt to meet with Bishop Páll and receive his letters, those destined for the archbishop. Then he went home to Hólar. Sigurðr then came from the east with Þuríðr and arranged with the candidate for bishop that their funds would not diminish, which they calculated at two hundred hundreds. That included all types of wealth, both livestock and chattels. That was agreed on.

29. Guðmundr Sets Sail

Guðmundr was ready to sail with his tithe resources. When he had got to the ship, Hrafn Sveinbjarnarson came from the west and was ready to travel with him as they had intended. Tómas Ragnheiðarson was also on hand along with Ívarr Jónsson, the monk Grímr, and Eyjólfr Snorrason. There were fifteen Icelanders. They weighed anchor the Sunday morning before the Dispersion of the Apostles (July 15, 1202).

The candidate for bishop had sent Kollsveinn Bjarnarson from his ship north along the fjord (Eyjafjǫrðr) to fetch his water casks, and Kollsveinn came from the north to the fjord when the ship had set sail. He was therefore left behind. Three men came rowing toward him, including Narfi from Brekka, and they had come from the east from Flatey with dried fish. Kollsveinn told them about his troubles and asked them for transportation. 'You're in a bad way,' said Narfi, 'and this is both crucial for you and the candidate for bishop. You should certainly be helped.'

They immediately unloaded their ship, took Kollsveinn and his freight on board, and rowed along the fjord under sail. The wind began to get stronger and the merchant ship made headway. Narfi spoke up when he saw that the merchant ship was pulling away: 'How long do we have to row after the merchantman for you to think that a proper effort has been made by us?' He answered: 'Out to the mouth of the fjord where the sea begins.' 'Fair enough,' said Narfi, 'and so shall it be.'

When the merchantman got out to Hrísey, the candidate for bishop said: 'Now we should lower the sail—I do not wish to abandon my man on land, and furthermore I want to celebrate Mass on the island today.' The Norwegians said that it was very much against their wishes to make no use of a good breeze. But Guðmundr said that this would be avenged—'and God will cause a greater delay of your voyage than this.'

When they saw that he was displeased, the sail was lowered and the anchor dropped. The candidate for bishop went ashore to celebrate Mass. Now Narfi and his companions no longer needed to row, and Kollsveinn embarked on the ship.

In the morning there was a breeze and they wanted to haul up their anchor, but it was stuck fast. One group after the other tried everything they could think of, but the anchor did not come up. The candidate for bishop was told about it. He approached and spoke a blessing and said: 'My Lord, free the anchor'—and he took hold of the rope. The anchor was freed, and they raised the sail and proceeded to Grímsey, where they lay at anchor for a week.

Then a breeze sprang up and they sailed north to Gnúpar. A contrary wind arose and drove them as far to the west as Skagi. Then they were righted and turned north again to Langanes. But a contrary wind sprang up again and drove them back on the sea to the west. Then one night on their ship a woman dreamed that a man in episcopal garb went along the ship to the place where the candidate for bishop was sleeping and spoke a blessing over him. He appeared to be Bishop Jón.

The following day the candidate for bishop spoke: 'It would be my advice to adjust the sail and proceed west around the land because north-east winds are blowing and there is no getting around the land to the north.' This advice was taken and they sailed to the west around the land and by the West Fjords and south to Snæfellsnes, then south to Reykjanes and on to Eyjafjǫll.

After that the north-east winds prevailed and drove them south where they sighted the Hebrides, which they recognised, and they arrived at the islands known as the Hirtir.[1] There they learned of the death of King Sverrir.

---

[1] The islands referred to here have not been identified.

Then they were carried south to the Irish Sea and south to Ireland. There was stormy weather, and they heard breakers in every direction around them.

Then the candidate for bishop said that everyone should make confession and the clerics attend to their tonsures and devise vows. It was done as he said. They vowed to give an ell from each bag of homespun and finance a pilgrim to Rome and each one give a fifth of a kilogram of wax to a church. Then the wind calmed down, and a breeze brought them to Norway, where the candidate for bishop went to meet King Hákon (Sverrisson) in Bergen.[1] He gave him a very good reception. The candidate for bishop sailed north to Trondheim and Archbishop Eiríkr consecrated him as bishop (April 13, 1203).

---

[1] Hákon Sverrisson was briefly King of Norway from 1202–1204. He appears in *Sverris saga*.

BIBLIOGRAPHY

TEXTS AND TRANSLATIONS

Biskupa sögur II. Ed. Ásdís Egilsdóttir. ÍF 16. Reykjavík: Hið Íslenzka Fornritafélag, 2002.
Byskupa sögur. Ed. Guðni Jónsson. Reykjavík: Íslendingasagnaútgáfan, 1953. 3 vols.
Biskupa sögur. Ed. Hið Íslenzka Bókmenntafélag. Copenhagen: S. L. Müller, 1858–1878. 2 vols.
Biskupa sögur I. Ed. Sigurgeir Steingrímsson, Ólafur Halldórsson, and Peter Foote. ÍF 15:1–2. Reykjavík: Hið Íslenzka Fornritafélag, 2003. 2 vols.
Byskupa sögur. Ed. Jón Helgason. Copenhagen: Editiones Arnamagnaeanae 13:1–2, 1938–1958. 2 vols.
Heilagra manna sögur: Fortællinger og legender om hellige mænd og kvinder. Ed. C. R. Unger. Christiania: B. M. Bentzen, 1877. 2 vols.
Heimskringla. Ed. Bjarni Aðalbjarnarson. ÍF 26–28. Reykjavík: Hið Íslenzka Fornritafélag, 1941–1951. 3 vols.
Heimskringla. Trans. Alison Finlay and Anthony Faulkes. [London]: Viking Society for Northern Research, University College London, 2011–2016. 3 vols.
Islandske Annaler indtil 1578. Ed. Gustav Storm. Det norske historiske kildeskriftsfonds skrifter, 21. Christiania: Grøndahl & Søns Boktrykkeri, 1888.
Islandske Annaler indtil 1578. Ed. Gustav Storm. Det norske historiske kildeskriftsfonds skrifter, 21. Christiania: Grøndahl & Søns Boktrykkeri, 1888.
Landnámabók. Ed. Jakob Benediktsson. ÍF 1.1–2. Reykjavík: Hið Íslenzka Fornritafélag. 1968. 2 vols.
Laxdæla saga. Ed. Einar Ól. Sveinsson. ÍF 5. Reykjavík: Hið Íslenzka Fornritafélag, 1934.
Monumenta Historica Norvegiae. Ed. Gustav Storm. Rpt. Oslo: Aas & Wahl Boktrykkeri, 1880; rpt. 1973.
Morkinskinna. Ed. Ármann Jakobsson and Þórður Ingi Guðjónsson. ÍF 23–24. Reykjavík: Hið Íslenzka Fornritafélag, 2011.
Morkinskinna. The Earliest Icelandic Chronicle of the Norwegian Kings (1030–1157). Trans. Theodore M. Andersson and Kari Ellen Gade. Islandica 51. Ithaca and London: Cornell University Press, 2000.

Njáls saga. Ed. Einar Ól. Sveinsson. ÍF 12. Reykjavík: Hið Íslenzka Fornritafélag, 1954.
Origines Islandicae: A Collection of the More Important Sagas and Other Native Writings Relating to the Settlement and Early History of Iceland. Ed. and trans. Gudbrand Vigfusson and F. York Powell. Oxford: Clarendon Press, 1905. 2 vols.
Orkneyinga saga. Ed. Finnbogi Guðmundsson. ÍF 34. Reykjavik: Hið Íslenzka Fornritafélag, 1965.
The Saga of Bishop Thorlak (Þorláks saga byskups). Trans. Ármann Jakobsson and David Clark. London: Viking Society for Northern Research, 2013.
The Saga of St. Jón of Hólar. Trans. Margaret Cormack, Introduction by Peter Foote. Tempe: ACMRS Press, 2021.
St. Gregory the Great: Pastoral Care. Trans. Henry Davis. New York: Newman Press, 1978.
Sturlunga saga. Ed. Jón Jóhannesson, Magnús Finnbogason, and Kristján Eldjárn. Reykjavík: Sturlungaútgáfan, 1946.
Sturlunga saga. Vol. 1: *The Saga of Hvamm-Sturla and The Saga of the Icelanders*. Trans. Julia H. McGrew; vol. 2: *Shorter Sagas of the Icelanders*. Trans. Julia H. McGrew and R. George Thomas. New York: Twayne Publishers and the American-Scandinavian Foundation, 1970–1974.
Sverris saga. Ed. Þorleifur Hauksson. ÍF 30. Reykjavík: Hið Íslenzka Fornritafélag, 2007.

STUDIES

Amundsen, Darrel W., and Carol Jean Diers. 1973. 'The Age of Menopause in Medieval Europe.' *Human Biology* 45:605–12.
Andersson, Theodore M. 2002. 'The Long Prose Form in Medieval Iceland.' *JEGP* 101:380–411.
Andersson, Theodore M. 2017. 'A Note on Conversation in the Sagas.' *Gripla* 28:227–235.
Ármann Jakobsson and Ásdís Egilsdóttir. 1998. 'Um Oddaverjaþátt.' *Goðasteinn* 34:134–143.
Ármann Jakobsson and Ásdís Egilsdóttir. 1999. 'Er Oddaverjaþætti treystandi?' *Ný Saga* 11:91–100.
Cucina, Carla. 2017. *Auðun e l'orso. Un racconto medievale islandese*. [Macerata]: eum edizioni Università di Macerata.

Dudden, F. Homes. 1967. *Gregory the Great: His Place in History and Thought.* New York: Russell & Russell. 2 vols.
Finnur Jónsson. 1920–1924. *Den oldnorske og oldislandske litteraturs historie.* Copenhagen: Gad. 3 vols. (*OOLH*)
Jón Böðvarsson. 1968. 'Munur eldri og yngri gerðar Þorláks sögu.' *Saga* 6:81–94.
Jón Helgason. 1976. 'Þorláks saga helga.' In *Kulturhistorisk leksikon.* Vol. 20:388–391.
Jónas Kristjánsson. 1988. *Eddas and Sagas: Iceland's Medieval Literature.* Trans. Peter Foote. Reykjavik: Hið Íslenzka Bókmenntafélag.
Kålund, P. E. Kristian. 1879–1882. *Bidrag til en historisk-topografisk beskrivelse af Island.* Copenhagen: Gyldendal. 2 vols.
Louis-Jensen, Jonna. 2006. 'Om roser og liljer.' In *Con Amore.* Ed. Michael Chesnutt and Florian Gammel. Copenhagen: C. A. Reitzels Forlag. 53–55.
Orri Vésteinsson. 2000. *The Christianization of Iceland: Priests, Power, and Social Change 1000–1300.* Oxford: Oxford University Press.
Sveinbjörn Rafnsson. 1993. *Páll Jónsson Skálholtsbiskup: Nokkrar athuganir á sögu hans og kirkjustjórn.* Ritsafn Sagnfræðistofunar 33. Reykjavík: Sagnfræðistofnun Háskóla Íslands.

INDEX OF PERSONAL NAMES

Absalon (archbishop) 40–41, 49, 61, 64
Account of the People at Oddi xiii
Adelbert (Archbishop of Bremen) 6–7
Agata Þorláksdóttir (abbess) 125
Agnes (saint) 105
Alexius Komnenus (emperor) 15
Ambrose (saint) 50, 105, 138, 141
Ámundi Árnason (architect) 44
Ámundi Árnason the Smith 52, 63
Ámundi Koðránsson 95
Anacletus II (pope) 26
Ambrosius saga byskups 141
Ari Bjarnarson 64, 101
Ari Eyjólfsson 77
Ari Másson 91
Ari Þorgilsson vii, 61, 91
Ármann Jakobsson viii, xx–xxi
Arngeirr Bǫðvarsson 93
Árni (architect) 28
Árni (priest) 21
Árni Ásbjargarson (bishop) 125
Árni rauðskeggr in Haukadalr 131
Árni at Skúmsstaðir 134–135
Árni Þorláksson (bishop) xx, xxv, 125
Arnórr Kolbeinsson 104, 111
Arnulf (patriarch in Jerusalem) 15
Arnþórr (married to Ragnheiðr Þórhallsdóttir) xx, 86
Arnþrúðr Fornadóttir at Vellir in Svarfaðardalr 124, 126, 128
Arons saga Hjǫrleifssonar xxvii
Ásbjǫrg Þorláksdóttir (nun) 125
Ásdís Egilsdóttir vii–viii, xiii, xviii, xx–xxi, xxvi, 5, 9, 21
Ásgeirr Gizurarson 16
Ásgrímr Vestliðason 100
Áskell (archbishop) 25, 27, 31
Ásmundr (a Norwegian) 105
Ásmundr kastanrassi 123–124
Asmundsen, Darrel xx
Atli (priest and book illuminator) 44
Bárðr (kinsman of Guðmundr Arason) 131
Bárðr sala 122–123
Bartholomew (saint) 139

INDEX OF NAMES 159

Battle at Fimreiti 115
Battle of Hastings 8
Battle at Íluvellir 105, 114
Beinir Sigurðarson 32
Benedict (brother of King Cnut) 17
Berghildr Þorvarðsdóttir 92
Bergþórr (lawspeaker) 21
Bergþórr Þórðarson 123
Bersi Halldórsson 64
Bersi Venison 109
Big Símon (priest) 147
Birna Brandsdóttir 92
Bjarnheðinn Sigurðarson 32
Bjarni (bishop in Orkney) 58
Bjarni Hallsson 114
Bjarnvarðr Vilráðsson (English bishop) x, 9
Bjǫrn (Auð-Bjǫrn) 120
Bjǫrn (priest) 55
Bjǫrn (Bishop Páll's chaplain) 53, 57
Bjǫrn bríkarnef 121–122
Bjǫrn bukkr 97
Bjǫrn the Marshall 97
Bjǫrn sterki 98
Bjǫrn Gilsson (abbot) 25, 27, 29–30, 98–99, 11
Bjǫrn Karlsefnisson 21
Bjǫrn Þorvaldsson (architect) 28
Book of Job xiii
Brandr Dálksson (priest) 55
Brandr Eyjólfsson 124, 126
Brandr Knakansson 92
Brandr Sæmundarson (bishop) xxxii–xxxiii, 30, 39, 42, 46, 49, 55, 64, 98–100, 103, 115–6, 119, 125–130, 136, 139
Brandr Tjǫrvason at Háls 93, 99, 101–2
Brandr Ǫnundarson 125
Brigid (saint) 20
Bǫðvarr Gizurarson 15–16
Bǫðvarr Grímsson 102
Bǫðvarr Þórðarson 76, 117
Cecilia (saint) 105
Celestine III (pope) 42, 61, 64
Clark, David viii
Cnut (Danish king) 17
Cnut Valdemarsson (Danish king) 41

Columbanus (saint) 6, 15
Cucina, Carla 6
Cura Pastoralis 20
Dalla Þorvaldsdóttir 5, 12–13
Darr-Þórir Þorvarðsson 93
Davis, Henry 20
Diers, Carol Jean xx
Dionysius 25
Dudden, Frederick H. 127
Efidius 139
Egidius 143
Einar Ól. Sveinsson xviii
Einarr opinsjóðr 98
Einarr Arason 91
Einarr Fork 139
Einarr Grímsson 103
Einarr Helgason 102
Einarr Jónsson 71
Einarr kati 116
Einarr Magnússon 22
Einarr Másson 64
Einarr nefja 107, 109
Einarr Þorgeirsson 91
Einarr Þorgilsson at Staðarhóll 103, 116
Eindriði (companion of Ǫgmundr Kálfsson) 122
Eiríkr (Danish archbishop) 40, 42, 49, 154
Eiríkr Hákonarson (from Orkney) 92
Eiríkr at Snorrastaðir 48
Eiríkr Sigurðarson (jarl and half-brother of King Sverrir) 124
Eldjárn (husband of Birna Brandsdóttir) 92
Erlingr (jarl) 94–97, 105
Eugenius III (pope)
Eyjólfr at Stafaholt xx, xxii, 74–77, 79
Eyjólfr at Vellir 124
Eyjólfr Einarsson 93
Eyjólfr Hallsson 140
Eyjólfr Jónsson 114
Eyjólfr Snorrason 151
Eyjólfr Sæmundarson 25
Eysteinn Erlendsson (archbishop) 30, 69, 73, 109, 117, 120, 123
Eysteinn Haraldsson (Norwegian king), 20–21, 31–32, 104
Finnr Hallsson (lawspeaker) 26
Finnur Jónsson viii, xxviii

INDEX OF NAMES

Friðrekr (visiting bishop) 8
Geirlaug Arnórsdóttir 74
Gelasius (pope) 20
Gellir Hǫskuldsson (priest) 115
Geoffrey of Monmouth 133
Gerlandus 8
Gils Hafsson 22
Gizurr the White 5
Gizurr Hallsson (lawspeaker) xxxiv, 3, 19, 27, 29, 31, 39, 43, 46, 49–50, 64, 111, 125–126, 134, 143
Gizurr Ísleifsson (bishop) viii–x, xii, 5, 10–20, 24, 61
Gregory I (pope) 16, 20, 116, 127
Gregory VII (pope) 11
Gríma Þorgeirsdóttir 93, 101
Grímr (monk) 151
Grímr Snorrason 93, 117
Gróa Gizurardóttir 15–16
Guðmundar saga Arasonar xviii
Guðmundar saga dýra 92, 124
Guðmundr Ámundason gríss 64, 125
Guðmundr Arason (bishop) ix, xvi, xxiv, xxvi–xxxiv, 46, 49, 55–58, 91, 93–94, 96, 98–99, 101–105, 107–112, 114–120, 123–142, 144–145, 148–152
Guðmundr Bjálfason (abbot), 64
Guðmundr Bjarnarson at Kleifar in Gilsfjǫrðr 112
Guðmundr Brandsson 25
Guðmundr inn dýri 143
Guðmundr kárhǫfði 94, 105
Guðmundr Ketilsson (priest) 32
Guðmundr Koðránsson 25
Guðni Jónsson xviii, xxv
Guðný Þorvarðsdóttir 92, 105
Guðrún Aradóttir 94
Guðrún Hreinsdóttir 75
Guðrún Sæmundardóttir (sister of Bishop Brandr) 116
Guðrún Þorláksdóttir at Kirkjubœr 125
Guðrún Þóroddsdóttir (Herdís Ketilsdóttir's niece) 53
Guðrún Þorvarðsdóttir 92
Gunnarr (a worker) 74
Gunnarr Arason 94
Gunnarr Helgason (Sledge-Gunnarr) 93
Gunnarr tjǫrskinn 98
Gunnlaugr Leifsson 133
Gunnlaugs saga xi

BISHOPS OF EARLY ICELAND

Guthormr Finnólfsson (priest) 7, 11
Gyðríðr Þorvarðsdóttir 92
Hafliði Másson 16, 21
Hafliði Þorvaldsson (abbot) 64
Hafr Brandsson (promotes Guðmundr Arason's candidacy) 143, 148
Hafr Svertingsson 22
Hafr-Bjǫrn Molda-Gnúpsson 22
Hákon herðibreiðr (Norwegian king) 32, 94–95, 99
Hákon Hákonarson (Norwegian king) xi
Hákon jarl (Norwegian ruler) 39
Hákon Magnússon 17
Hákon Sverrisson (Norwegian king) 49, 58, 64, 154
Halla Pálsdóttir xiii, xv–xvi, xviii, 38, 52–53
Hallbera Einarsdóttir 91, 105
Hallbera Þorvarðsdóttir 92
Halldóra Brandsdóttir 71
Halldóra Eyjólfsdóttir (mother of Bishop Klœngr) 27, 126
Halldóra Hrólfsdóttir 5
Halldórr Hallvarðsson (priest) 140
Halldórr Jónsson 71
Halldórr Snorrason 95
Hallfríðr Ófeigsdóttir 123
Hallfríðr Snorradóttir 17
Hallgerðr Runólfsdóttir 104
Hallr Gizurarson 49, 150
Hallr Gizurarson (error for Gizurr Hallsson) 39
Hallr Hrafnsson 103, 124
Hallr Teitsson 19, 25–26
Hallsteinn (steersman) 107
Hallsteinn kúlubakr 105
Haraldr (jarl in Orkney) 37, 64
Haraldr gilli Magnússon (Norwegian king) 22–23, 32, 96
Haraldr Sigurðarson (Norwegian king) 8–11, 15–16
Harðvík/Hartwig (Archbishop of Magdeburg) 11–12
Harold Godwinson 10
Hávarðr (ship captain) 105–106
Heðinn Eilífsson 93
Heimskringla 10, 22, 95, 99, 102, 104
Heinrekr (bishop) 9
Heinrich (emperor) 6
Helga (mother of Ǫgmundr Þorvarðsson) 92
Helga Þorvarðsdóttir 92
Helgi Eiríksson 93

INDEX OF NAMES 163

Helgi Skaptason 32, 103–104
Helgi Skeljungsson (priest) 110
Helgi Þórðarson 93
Helgi Ǫgmundarson (bishop in Greenland) 116
Henry I (English king) 26
Herdís Ketilsdóttir xiii, xvi–xix, 37–38, 43, 51–54
Herdís Klœngsdóttir 92
Herdís Sighvatsdóttir 92
Hermundr Koðránsson 64, 75
Hesthǫfði Guðrúnarson 116
Hjálmr Ásbjarnarson 92, 143
Hjalti Skeggjason 5
Hrafn Sveinbjarnarson 146–147, 151
Hrafn Úlfheðinsson (lawspeaker) 26
Hreinn (abbot) 32, 100
Hreinn Hermundarson 74—75
Hrói (bishop in the Faroe Islands) 100
Hungrvaka vii–viii, x, xii–xiii, xxix–xxx, xxxiv, 3
Húnrǫðr (nephew of Jón Húnrǫðarson) 114
Hvamm-Sturla 93, 98
Hǫgni Þormóðsson at Bœr xxii–xxiii, 74–75, 77, 79, 113
Hǫskuldr Herason 102
Illugi Leifsson 28
Ingi (claimant to the Norwegian throne), 58
Ingi Haraldsson (Norwegian king) 32, 91, 94, 98, 120
Ingibjǫrg Þorgeirsdóttir 93, 110
Ingibjǫrg Þorvarðsdóttir 92
Ingimundr Grímsson 15
Ingimundr Jónsson, 102–103
Ingimundr Þorgeirsson 93, 96–97, 101–108, 110–113, 116–117, 119–123
Ingjaldr (kinsman of Sturla Þórðarson) 103
Ísleifr Gizurarson (bishop) viii–xii, 4–8, 10–11, 13
Íslendingabók vii
Íslendinga saga xxix, xxxii
Ívarr dœlski 98
Ívarr gilli 97
Ívarr Jónsson 151
Job xiii, xvi
John the Baptist 87, 138
Jón (Irish bishop) x, 8
Jón (bishop in Greenland) 48, 64, 117, 120
Jón fjósi 98
Jón (follower of King Ingi) 91–92

Jón Brandsson 110–111, 133
Jón Birgisson (archbishop) 32
Jón Bǫðvarsson xx–xxi
Jón Gizurarson 16
Jón Helgason xxv
Jón Húnrǫðarson 12, 114–115
Jón Ketilsson (brother of Herdís Ketilsdóttir) xviii–xix, 53
Jón Ketilsson (priest) xviii
Jón kuflungr 116, 120–121, 123
Jón Loptsson xv, xx, xxii–xxv, 29–30, 39, 43, 45, 62, 64, 70–73, 81–87
Jón Sigmundarson 32, 100, 136, 139
Jón Ǫgmundrson (bishop) xxxiii, 7, 13, 19, 21, 41, 49, 128–129, 137–38, 153
Jónas Kristjánsson xxvii
Jóns saga helga vii, xiii, xxx–xxxi
Kålund, P. E. Kristian 9
Kálfr Snorrason 64
Kári (abbot) 120
Karl Jónsson (abbot) 102–3, 116, 133
Kárr Koðránsson 102
Ketilbjǫrg (nun) xxxiv, 134
Ketilbjǫrn the Old 4
Ketill at Grund 103
Ketill Gizurarson 5
Ketill Hermundarson (priest) 55
Ketill Kálfsson 91
Ketill Ketilsson (brother of Herdís Ketilsdóttir) xv
Ketill Pálsson xv–xvi, 38, 52–53
Ketill Þorsteinson (bishop) 15, 19, 24, 27
Klemet Arason 93
Klœngr Eyjólfsson 124, 126
Klœngr Kleppjárnsson 92
Klœngr Þorsteinsson (bishop) 16, 27, 29–32, 98, 104
Klœngr Þorvaldsson (chieftain) 60
Knútr (Swedish king) 64
Kolbeinn Arnórsson at Staðr 128
Kolbeinn Tumason xxix–xxx, xxxii–xxxiii, 56–57, 92, 128–129, 134–5, 139–140, 143–46, 148
Kolli Þorláksson 93
Kolli Þormóðsson 93
Koll-Oddr 112, 114–115
Kollsveinn Bjarnarson 152–153
Kolr (bishop) 7–8
Kolr (bishop in Norway) 7

Kolr (Norwegian bell maker) 44
Konrad (emperor) 6
Kygri-Bjǫrn Hjaltason xxviii, 145
Lambert (bishop) 21
Lamkárr Þorgilsson xxvii–xxviii, 140, 145
Landnámabók xv, xviii
Liemar (archbishop) 11
Laxdæla saga xxiii
Leggr (priest) 55
Loptr Pálsson xv–xvi, xviii, 38, 52, 58
Louis-Jensen, Jonna xxvi
McGrew, Julia H. xxix, 16, 102–103
Magnús (priest) xxiii, 77
Magnús (saint) 17
Magnús Ámundason 109, 11
Magnús Bareleg (Norwegian king) 17, 37
Magnús Erlingsson (Norwegian king) 95, 99 105, 115, 121
Magnús the Good (Norwegian king) 9–10
Magnús Einarsson (bishop) viii–xi, 22–26
Magnús Gizurarson (candidate for bishop) xxxii, 46, 49, 61, 126, 143, 150
Magnús Guðmundarson (goði) 125
Magnús Sigurðarson (Norwegian king) 22, 26
Magnús Þórðarson 22
Magnús Þorláksson (canon) 125
Magnús Þorsteinsson 22
Margrét the Cunning (carver) 59
Már Finnsson 124
Markús Skeggjason 12, 17
Markús Þórðarson 76
Martin (bishop at Tours) 137
Matthew (saint) 129, 131
Michael (archangel) 138
Morkinskinna 10, 22, 26, 92
Narfi from Brekka 152
Nicholas (abbot) 29
Nicholas the Saint 17, 134
Nicholaus Sigurðarson 32
Nikulás (Norwegian bishop) 59
Nikulás Sigurðarson 104
Njáll (bishop) 64
Njáls saga xi, xxi
Oddaverja þáttr xix–xxvii
Oddný Magnússdóttir 22

Oddný Þorgeirsdóttir 93
Oddr Gizurarson 111
Óláfr Guðbrandsson 96
Óláfr Haraldsson (Saint Óláfr) 9–10, 138, 142–143
Óláfr kyrri (Norwegian king) 15, 17
Óláfr Magnússon (Norwegian king) 17
Óláfr Tryggvason (Norwegian king) 133
Óláfr Þorsteinsson 105
Ólǫf Eyjólfsdóttir 77
Orkneyinga saga 37
Ormr (chaplain of Bishop Þorlákr) 84–85
Ormr the Old 70
Ormr Jónsson 71, 126
Ormr Loptsson 43, 46, 49
Ormr Þorláksson (canon) 125
Orri Vésteinsson xxi, xxviii, 13
Páll (Burnt Páll) 104
Páll Jónsson (bishop) xiii, xv–xx, xxviii, xxxiv, 37–64, 71, 125–126, 128, 131–132, 134, 149–151
Páll Sǫlvason 25
Páll Þórðarson 32, 100, 103
Páls saga byskups xiii, xvi–xvii, xix, xxvi, xxx, 8
Paschal II (pope) 13, 15
Patrick (Irish saint) xii, 33
Paul (saint) 138
Peter (saint) 12, 28–29, 62, 138
Pétr (Danish bishop) 42
Pétr glyfsa 122–123
Philip I (French king) 15
Philippus (jarl) 64
Prestssaga Guðmundar góða ix, xxviii–xxxi, xxxiv
The Priesthood of Guðmundr the Good xiii
Prophecies of Merlin 133
Ragnheiðr Þórhallsdóttir xx, 37, 71, 81, 86–87
Rannveig Úlfheðinsdóttir 93
Remigius (saint) 126
Richard I (English king) 64
Rúðólfr (bishop from Rouen) x, 9
Runólfr Ketilsson 28
Runólfr Þorláksson 17
Rǫgnvaldr (jarl) 37
Sigfúss Grímsson (priest) 53
Sigmundr Ormsson 64

INDEX OF NAMES

Sigríðr (wife of Tumi at Áss) 103
Sigríðr Eldjárnsdóttir at Espihóll 92
Sigríðr Tumadóttir 93, 103
Sigríðr Úlfheðinsdóttir 93
Sigurðr Hávarsson af Reyri (jarl) 95
Sigurðr Jónsson 71
Sigurðr Jórsalafari (Norwegian king) 20–21, 31–32
Sigurðr Ormsson xxviii–xxix, xxxii–xxxiii 68–69, 127, 135, 138, 148–151
Sigurðr slembidjákn (Norwegian king) 26, 92
Simon (apostle) 23
Snorri at Skálavík 132–133
Snorri the Chieftain 10
Snorri Arngeirsson (a healer) 110
Snorri Grímsson 125
Snorri Kálfsson 102, 104
Snorri Karlsefnisson 17
Snorri Snorrason 124
Snorri Sturluson xxx, xxxiii, 77, 129
Snorri Svertingsson 25
Snorri Þórðarson 100, 126
Snælaug Hǫgnadóttir 74–77, 79, 113
Steini (priest) 76
Steinn (priest) 137
Steinunn Sturludóttir 110
Steinunn Þorgrímsdóttir 10, 13–14
Steinunn Þorsteinsdóttir 93
Steinþórr at Eyrr 93
Steinþórr Bjarnarson 131
Sturla Bárðarson 140
Sturla Þórðarson xxix, 103, 113–114
Sturlu saga 102–103, 113
Sturlunga saga xxix–xxx, 16, 92, 100, 102–103, 124
Styrkárr Oddason (lawspeaker) 103, 111
Styrkárr Sigmundarson 91
Sumarliði Ásmundarson 125
Sunnifa (saint) 103
Sveinbjörn Rafnsson xviii, 50
Sveinn Sturluson xxii, 80, 103–104
Sveinn Úlfsson (Danish king) 10
Sverrir Sigurðarson (Norwegian king) xi, xv, 37, 40, 42, 48, 61,64, 104–105, 114, 124, 153
Sverris saga 105, 115–116, 133, 154
Svertingr Hafr-Bjarnarson 22

Sæmundr Brandsson 71
Sæmundr Jónsson xxviii–xxix, 50, 88, 136, 149–150
Sæmundr Loptsson 43, 46, 49
Sæmundr Sigfússon xi, 12, 21, 37, 72
Sǫrkvir (Swedish king) 64
Teitr Ísleifsson 5, 16–17
Teitr Ketilbjarnarson 4
Teitr Oddsson 92, 140
Thomas (English archbishop and saint) 32, 102
Thomas, R. George 124
Tjǫrvi Bǫðvarsson 19, 25
Tómas Ragnheiðarson 151
Tumi Kolbeinsson at Áss 103
Úlfheðinn Kollason 93
Úlfheiðr Gunnarsdóttir 93–94, 96, 129
Úlfr (alternative name for Bishop Rúðólfr) 9
Úlfrún (anchorite) 147
Valdimarr Knútsson (Danish king) 111
Valgerðr Hallgerðardóttir 104
Vilborg Gizurardóttir 5
Vilmundr Snorrason 102
William the Conqueror 17
Yngvildr Þorgilsdóttir 92
Þóra (mother of Jón Loptsson) 37
Þóra Pálsdóttir xv–xvi, 38, 52
Þóra Þorgeirsdóttir 93
Þórálfr Snorrason (priest) 116
Þórarinn rosti 108–109
Þórarinn at Staðr 105
Þórarinn the Steward 145–146
Þórarinn Þorkelsson skotakolls 17
Þorbjǫrn Hops 107
Þórdís (wife of Gizurr the White) 5
Þórdís Þóroddsdóttir 5
Þórðr Crow 107
Þórðr Arason 130
Þórðr Bǫðvarsson (priest) 74–77, 79, 113
Þórðr Gizurarson 16
Þórðr Ívarsson 114–115, 123
Þórðr Vermundarson 146
Þórðr Þorgeirsson 92
Þórðr Ǫnundarson 92
Þórðr Snorrason 64

INDEX OF NAMES 169

Þorfinnr Þorgeirsson (abbot) 115
Þorgeirr Brandsson xxxii, 92, 105, 115, 117–118
Þorgeirr Hallason 91, 99–102
Þorgerðr Þorláksdóttir at Kirkjubœr 125
Þorgils Arason 91
Þorgils Gunnsteinsson 130
Þorgils Oddason 21, 92
Þorgils saga ok Hafliða xxvii, 16
Þorgrímr alikarl 114
Þórir (Bishop Páll Jónsson's treasurer) xviii, 59–60
Þórir Arngeirsson 93
Þórir Broddason 10
Þórir Símunarson 21
Þórir Steinmóðsson 26
Þórir víkverski (Norwegian archbishop) xvii, 41, 59
Þorkatla Skaptadóttir 5
Þorkell hagi 98
Þorkell Eiríksson 116
Þorkell Eyjólfsson 10
Þorkell Flosason 100
Þorkell Hallsson 39, 55
Þorkell Skúmsson (abbot) 64
Þorlákr Ketilsson (brother of Herdís Ketilsdóttir) xviii, xix, 46, 54
Þorlákr Magnússon 125
Þorlákr Runólfsson (bishop) ix–x, xii–xiii, 14, 17–22, 25
Þorlákr Þórarinsson 17
Þorlákr Þórhallsson (bishop) viii, xii, xvii, xix–xxvi, xxxiii, 31–33, 37–39, 43–47, 51,61, 67–68, 70–71, 73, 75, 77, 79–85, 87–88, 105, 111–113, 124–126, 128–129, 137
Þorláks saga byskups vii–viii, xiii, xxvi, xxx–xxxi
Þorleifr beiskaldi 76–77, 79
Þorleifr Þórðarson 76
Þorleifr Þorláksson 46, 64
Þormóðr Kollason 93
Þórný Aradóttir 93
Þórný Þorgeirsdóttir 93
Þóroddr (worker for Þórðr Ívarsson) 114
Þóroddr Jórsalamaðr 98
Þorsteinn (goldsmith) 47
Þorsteinn (deacon) 53
Þorsteinn (a cabinet maker) 59, 60
Þorsteinn Eiríksson 116
Þorsteinn Hallsson af Siðu 22

Þorsteinn Hallvarðsson 21
Þorsteinn Jónsson xxii–xxiii, 71, 81–83, 87
Þorsteinn Kuggason 10
Þorsteinn Snorrason 124
Þorsteinn Tumason (abbot) 111
Þorsteinn Þraslaugarson 127
Þorvaldr (a chieftain) 5
Þorvaldr the Wealthy 100
Þorvaldr Gizurarson 46, 49, 51, 61–62, 125–126, 150
Þorvaldr Þorgilsson 64
Þorvarðr Ásgrímsson 117
Þorvarðr Þorgeirsson (grandfather of Guðmundr Arason) 91–92, 94–95, 101–104, 111, 120, 141–144
Þuríðr (companion of Árni rauðskeggr) 131
Þuríðr (mother of Kolbeinn Tumason) xxix, xxxii
Þuríðr Gilsdóttir 22
Þuríðr Gizurardóttir (wife of Sigurðr Ormsson) 148, 151
Ǫgmundr Kálfsson (abbot) 111, 120–123
Ǫgmundr rafakollr 116
Ǫgmundr Þorvarðsson 102, 116, 120, 141
Ǫnundr Þorkelsson 64, 124
Ǫrn (slain by Sveinn Sturluson) 80
Ǫzurr (archbishop at Lund) 13–14, 18–19, 23, 26

INDEX OF PLACE NAMES

Árnes 24
Ásgeirsá 116
Áss 5
Bakki (in Miðfjǫrðr) 115
Bari 17, 27
Bergen 10, 42, 91, 120, 130, 154
Bielefeld 5
Blǫndubakki 134
Blǫnduóss 22
Borgarfjǫrðr 5, 9, 18, 74, 129
Breiðabólstaðr 71, 110–112, 126
Breiðafjǫrðr 130
Brodddanes 133
Bœr xxiii, 74–77, 79
Cologne 99, 145
Dalir 112
Denmark 10, 19, 22–23, 40–41, 49
Drangar 110
England 9–10, 37, 120
Eyjafjǫll 16, 135, 153
Eyjafjǫrðr 5, 23, 42, 91, 93, 95, 116–117, 128–129, 134, 140, 152
Eyjar 81
Fagradalr 129
Fellsmúli 83
Flatey 130, 134, 152
Fljótsdalr 92, 128, 139
Fljótshlíð 25, 126
Flói 100
Fyrileif 22
Garðar on Akranes 74, 76
Gásir 95, 105, 126
Geitdalr 116
Geitland 5
Giljá 9
Gilsbakki 74
Gnúpar 105, 153
Greenland 6, 91, 123
Grenjaðarstaðir 103–104, 140
Grímsá 76
Grímsey 153
Grímsnes 100

Grjótá 93, 98
Grund 103, 126
Gunnarsholt 81
Hallormsstaðir 70
Háls 101, 103, 105, 111–112, 141
Hamarkaupangr 95
Hamarr 41
Haukadalr x, 5, 17, 19, 127, 131
Hebrides 153
Hegranes 101
Hekla 32, 50, 64
Heklufell 17
Helgafell 104
Herford xi, 5
Herjólfsnes 91
Herrevad 41
Hirtir (unidentified islands) 153
Hítardalr 25–26, 60, 76
Hjalli 5
Hjaltadalr (in Skagafjǫrðr) 14
Hjǫrleifshǫfði 70
Hlíð 139
Hof (in Skagafjǫrðr) 93, 117–118, 132, 140
Hof (in Vápnafjǫrðr) 10
Hólar xvi, xxvii, xxviii, xxx, 7, 14, 19, 21, 25, 27, 30, 41, 46, 49, 58, 93, 98–99, 117, 119, 130, 144–45, 147–148, 151
Hornstrandir 105, 108
Hrafnabjǫrg 95
Hraungerði 5
Hrísey 152
Húnafjǫrðr 5, 9
Hvammr xxxiii, 113, 129
Hvassafell (in Eyjafjǫrðr) 91, 96, 101
Hvítá 112
Hǫfðá 71–72
Hǫfðabrekkuland 71
Hǫfðastrǫnd 93
Hǫrgardalr 93
Ireland 17, 33, 154
Ísafjǫrðr 131
Kálfanes 111
Kálfstaðir 145
Keldudalr 130

INDEX OF NAMES

Keldur 87
Kirkjubœr xxxiii, 126
Kjarnes 115
Klofi 84
Krossavík 139
Langadalr 134
Langahlíð 93
Langanes 153
Laufás 101, 128
Laugardalr 7
Laugaráss 24
Leirubakki 83
Ljósavatn 101
Lómagnúpr 135
Lómagnúpssandr 68
Maastricht 21
Málmey 108
Marbœli 123
Melrakkaslétta 105
Miðfjǫrðr 114, 129, 132, 146–147
Miklabœr 120, 123–124
Mosfell 4
Múli 77
Munkaþverá 99, 101
Mǫðrudalsheiðr 140
Mǫðruvellir 99, 102, 115
Niðaróss 40
Nordrheinwestfalen 5
Oddi xx, xxix, 38–39, 70–71
Odense 17
Orkney 37, 92
Rangá 81
Rangáróss 11
Rangárvellir 81
Rauðalœkr 70
Raumsdalr 95
Ré 104
Reykjahólar 110, 129
Reykjaholt xxiii, 18, 25, 77
Reykjanes 91, 93, 110, 130, 153
Reykjarfjǫrðr 80, 109
Reyrr 95
Rome 9, 11, 16, 27, 48, 106, 154

Roskilde 42
Rouen 9
Ryðjǫkull 97
Sakka (in Svarfaðardalr) 126
Sandártunga 24
Sarpsborg 23
Sauðlausdalr 130
Saurbœr (unspecified) 112
Saurbœr (in Eyjafjǫrðr) 105
Saurbœr (on Hvalfjarðarstrand) 74, 102
Saurbœr (on Kjalarnes) 103
Saxony 6, 10–12
Sekkr 95, 99
Selja 8, 10, 24, 39, 60, 103
Síða 135
Skagafjǫrðr 101, 103, 139, 140
Skagi 153
Skálaholt vii–viii, xiv, xviii, 3–8, 12–13, 16, 18–19, 22, 24–25, 27, 29, 39, 42–44, 48, 52, 59–61, 98, 125, 128, 149–151
Skálavík 132
Skarð 38, 40, 52–53
Skjalda-Bjarnarvík 108
Snæfellsnes 153
Sogn 115
Staðarbakki 147
Staðarhóll 112
Staðr (in Skagafjǫrðr) 104–105, 116–117, 128
Stafafell 139
Steingrímsfjǫrðr 110–111, 129, 132
Steinsstaðir 9
Strandir 109, 111, 118
Súðavík 131
Svarfaðardalr xxxiii, 139
Sveinsstaðir 9
Svínafell xxix, 68, 70, 127–128, 135, 138, 148
Svínavatn 104
Sælingsdalsheiðr 103, 113
Trondheim 10, 32, 49, 117, 142, 154
Túnsberg 94
Ufsir 127–128
Ulster 17
Upplǫnd 95
Utrecht 26

Vaglar 102
Valþjófsstaðir 139
Vápnafjǫrðr 128, 139
Vatnsdalr 5, 9, 132
Vatnsendi 114
Vatnsfjǫrðr 100, 103, 132
Vellir 83, 124–127, 139
Ver 40, 135
Vestmannaeyjar 24, 53
Víðey 125
Víðimýrr 128–129, 134, 141, 144
Víðivellir (in Skagafjǫrðr) xxxii–xxxiii, 93, 116, 143
Víðvík 124
Vík 94, 97, 124
Wendland 9
West Fjords 25, 60, 80, 111, 126, 130–131, 147, 153
Ytra-Skarð 71, 84
Þaralátrsfjǫrðr 108
Þingeyrar xxxiii, 102, 111, 114, 133, 143, 147
Þingvellir 16
Þorkelshváll 114
Þverá 99, 111, 143
Þjórsá 52
Þváttá 70
Þverá 92, 99, 111, 143
Þykkvabœr 31, 40, 125
Ǫllfus 5
Øxarfjǫrðr 128, 140